SPINELESS

SPINELESS

BY

SAMANTHA SAN MIGUEL

union
square
kids

NEW YORK

union square kids

NEW YORK

Text © 2022 Samantha San Miguel
Cover art © 2022 Jamie Green

ISBN 978-1-4549-3762-3 (HC-PLC)
ISBN 978-1-4549-3763-0 (e-book)

Library of Congress Control Number: 2022930990

For information about custom editions, special sales, and premium purchases,
please contact specialsales@unionsquareandco.com.

Printed in Canada

Lot #:
2 4 6 8 10 9 7 5 3 1
04/22

unionsquareandco.com

Design by Julie Robine

To Johnny, since he asked first.

To the rest of my siblings:
try again next time, you slowpokes.

CHAPTER

1

THE BOOK SKIDDED across the deck and scattered Algie's shuffleboard game.

Like many twelve-year-olds, Algie Emsworth was used to his older brother's dramatics. "You didn't like *Twenty Thousand Leagues Under the Sea?*" he asked, retrieving the book and smoothing its pages.

"Someone should take that publisher to court for false advertising. Maybe I'll do it myself!" Sixteen-year-old Everett jabbed a finger at the front cover, which showed tentacles roiling from an inky sea, and a squid's eye bulging as it attempted to ram the *Nautilus* submarine down its beak. "Almost three hundred pages, and only two about the giant squid! Why didn't you warn me?"

"I did," Algie said. "When you borrowed it."

"Did you? Hmm. I must not have been listening." Everett went to the rail and squinted across at the white line of sand dunes off the steamer boat's port bow. A group of passengers trickled by on the deck: ladies with parasols and sweeping skirts, and perspiring gentlemen in coats and Panama hats. One man stopped to aim a pair of binoculars shoreward.

"Another dead one?" asked the lady beside him.

"We're taking the next boat home," the man grumbled. "What sort of health resort has a beach lined with carcasses?"

"We're not at the Hotel Paraíso yet," soothed the lady. "I'm sure they'll have an explanation."

Algie stowed *Twenty Thousand Leagues* in his knapsack as the group moved off. He took out his spyglass and climbed onto the rail beside Everett. Onshore, waves foamed around a lifeless heap. It was a small whale. Pulling out his field notebook, Algie balanced it against the railing and wrote:

> *"The carcasses have increased in frequency all afternoon as we near our destination. I have seen dead manatees, whales, and dolphins, as well as piles of dead fish. Several unidentifiable flesh blobs have also been noted. Could they be decayed portions of larger animals, or a yet-unclassified species?"*

"Is this normal, do you think?" Everett shaded his eyes against the sparkle.

"I don't know," Algie said. "But I'm going to find out."

Despite the warm breeze, goose bumps prickled Algie's arms as he recalled those featureless mounds of flesh. He sneezed three times and adjusted his umbrella hat. He always felt safer with it in place.

"I wish you wouldn't wear that ridiculous thing everywhere." Everett shot a disgusted look at Algie's headgear.

"Professor Champion says an umbrella hat is indispensable in any tropical latitude," said Algie, with dignity. "It performs many useful functions such as water baler, sunshade, and deflector of poisonous darts. A good naturalist doesn't care about looking ridiculous in the name of science." The hat, consisting of a miniature umbrella canopy and removable length of mosquito net, was Algie's pride and joy. He had built it according to the description in Professor Ransom Champion's, "A Gentleman's Journey to Komodo," from the October issue of the *Youth's Companion*.

"Yes, but you aren't a good naturalist," Everett said. "Or even a bad one."

"Not yet." Algie sneezed again and drew himself to his full height of four feet, ten and three-quarters inches. "Even Professor Champion had to start somewhere. I'm starting here."

Everett snorted. "Yes, and whose fault is it that we're here?" Ever since their mother had announced they would be wintering at a health resort in Florida, his moods had grown more erratic, swinging from helpful to irritable.

"It's not my fault I have asthma." Algie wiped his watering nose. His sneezes had been worsening all day, along with the

9

dead sea creatures. He hoped he wasn't headed for an asthma attack.

"It's all right for you," Everett said. "You're too sick to go to school or play sports. But I get yanked from my college prep because Mother thinks I'll develop typhoid, or—or galloping consumption the minute she turns her back—"

"She's afraid of losing us," Algie said. "Like we lost Father."

Everett's jaw turned bulldoggish, the way it always did at the mention of Father.

"And a lot of good it did," he said, "having him close by." Their father had died of tuberculosis three years ago.

Algie bit the inside of his cheek. He understood Everett hadn't wanted to come to Florida. But it was hard to sympathize, because he himself was ecstatic. Gone were the days of scribbling treatises on "The Social Life of Lincoln Park Squirrels," and "Stringfoot in the Chicago Street Pigeon." In Chicago's frozen white avenues, with cable cars rattling up and down and the sun slinking below the horizon before dinnertime, the Hotel Paraíso's promotional brochure had read like pages from a sunlit fairy tale. "Underwater gardens—salubrious clime—every modern convenience in the subtropical jungle!"

Algie remembered looking up the word "salubrious" in the library at the Chicago Academy of Natural History. "Salubrious—healthy, wholesome, favorable to the health." He'd looked out the window at the falling snow, breathed a lungful of dry air, and coughed.

There were six weeks left in the hotel season. Algie had six weeks to make a scientific discovery that would prove to the Academy he was a force to be reckoned with. No more rejected research papers. No more notices informing him that, "The Chicago Academy of Natural History does not accept underage members." Algie couldn't afford to wait until he grew up. As the nineteenth century drew to a close, medical breakthroughs had become almost commonplace, but asthma could still be a death sentence. And there was the ever-present fear, the one his mother never voiced—the real reason she had brought him to South-west Florida and its healing climate—the possibility that Algie's breathing problems were not merely asthma, but the same deadly tuberculosis that had stolen his father.

"All right, darlings?" Mrs. Emsworth asked, pausing in her stroll around the deck. "Algie, you look pale. Why don't you rest in your cabin until we arrive?"

"Of course he's pale," Everett said, while Algie escaped from the frilly sunshade his mother attempted to hold over him. "He's been stuck inside all winter. Finish your walk, Mother. I'll look after Algie."

"Will you really?" Algie asked, as Mrs. Emsworth smiled at her eldest son and moved off. "Look after me, I mean?" In Chicago, Everett never had much time for him.

"I don't know." Everett propped his forearms against the rail. "Are you planning on getting into trouble?"

"*Yes.*" Algie thought of Professor Champion's adventures. He shut his eyes, smelling steam coal and ladies' perfume, and an odd, tangy brine so sharp it stung his throat. He heard the *pfft* of a manatee clearing its nostrils, and Everett biting his thumbnail. In his mind he saw the blue-green ocean, dotted with seaweed and the pinky-transparent outlines of cannonball jellyfish. All of Algie's senses were heightened. The reverse side of serious illness was that no matter how hard he tried, he could not take his breaths for granted. And at the end of the day, that was a good thing.

"Is that the hotel's pier?" Everett asked.

Algie opened his eyes, and black spots danced across his vision where the sun glanced off the breakers. Something seemed to pulse through the water.

He blinked. He looked again.

"Everett?" he said.

"Yes?"

"Is there an enormous yellow eye looking up out of the ocean?"

Everett peered over the side.

"No," he said.

Algie nodded, reassured. Yes, it was an ordinary ocean now, lapping the barnacle-studded pier. No black-barred pupil. No otherworldly gaze.

Still . . .

"When did you last take your medicine?" Everett asked.

"This morning," Algie said. It was true his asthma medicine made him see funny things occasionally, but the effects never lasted this long. Besides, that eyeball had been clear and defined, not hazy and surreal.

12

"Everett," Algie said, "I don't think it was the medicine."

His brother wasn't listening.

"Look," he said. "They've caught something."

Two gentlemen lounged in a fishing skiff by the deep-water pier. One sported a jaunty yachting cap, the other a safari helmet and luxuriant side-whiskers. The man in the cap was reeling in his line. Soon a dark shape could be seen dragging through the water.

"What's that?" Everett shaded his eyes. "A cuttlefish?"

"A little octopus," Algie said, as the side-whiskered man in the boat said, "Octopus. Half-dead, by the looks of it."

The football-sized creature did look as though it could use a pick-me-up, or at least a cup of tea. Whitish grey, its arms hung limp as it gazed at its captors through huge, mournful eyes.

"They eat these fellows in Japan." The whiskered man picked up the octopus and jerked the fishhook out of its mantle. "And in the Maldive Islands. Quite a delicacy."

"Any good?" the capped man asked.

"Not to my taste. We'll cut off its arms for bait," the second man decided. "No—maybe leave it one or two and use the body first. It'll look tastier alive and wriggling."

"That's not very sportsmanlike," said Everett. Algie couldn't say anything. He gripped the railing, the sunbaked metal burning his palms.

"Ouch!" the first man yelled and dropped the octopus. "It bit me!"

"Not so fast," said the side-burned man, prying the octopus off the side of the boat as it made a break for freedom. "Accept your fate philosophically—OW!"

The octopus turned bright red. Lashing out with its arms, it snatched the man's safari helmet and flung it into the sea. Gold-rimmed spectacles followed, and then a whole luxuriant sideburn floated in the waves.

Algie and Everett cheered.

The man in the yachting cap goggled. "I didn't know you wore false whiskers."

"Well, I do!" the other man roared, shooting a furious look at the boys on the steamer. "And they're bloody expensive too!" Ripping the octopus away from his chest, he squeezed the little animal with both hands. The octopus writhed and tugged at the man's wrists but could not pry itself free. Its color went from red to blue, and then began to drain back to grey.

"Stop it!" Algie yelled.

"Is it dead?" the man in the yachting cap asked.

"Not yet." The other man chomped on his mustache. "I'm going to turn it inside out and rip out its giblets."

"No!" Algie shouted and jumped overboard.

CHAPTER

2

KOOSH. **BUBBLES FIZZED** past Algie's face.

Scissor-kick with the legs and sweep with the arms—so his books on swimming had instructed. Algie kicked and swept.

But he did not shoot to the surface and speed through the water. The ocean had been more buoyant in his imagination. Algie kicked harder as panic swelled his throat. His lungs heaved against his rib muscles. Salt burned his eyes as he looked up at his own plume of bubbles against the backlit surface and the receding splotch of the fishing skiff. Salt was everywhere—in the corners of his mouth, stinging his lips and nose.

Algie thrashed harder as fear overwhelmed his limbs. The sun was a hazy globe in a blue-green sky. He always knew he would die gulping for air . . .

A noise like a dull explosion, and Algie was seized by his collar and towed upward, sparkles popping across his vision. His head broke water, into sound and oxygen and wet hair plastered over his eyes.

"I'm going to murder you!" Everett shouted in his ear.

"Hold hard," a voice called as the fishing skiff drew alongside. Strong hands gripped his shoulders.

Algie landed on his back in the bottom of the skiff. The boat tilted as Everett climbed inside, then righted with a jerk that bumped Algie's nose into a picnic basket and sent a half-eaten watercress sandwich toppling onto his head.

"What do you think you're playing at?" barked the octopus captor, who had recovered his safari helmet. A string of seaweed dangled from his ear.

The octopus—Algie's stomach clenched with dread. He was afraid to look at the limp white form dangling from the man's hand. Was he too late? Was it a living creature still, or an inside-out lump of bait? He forced a look. The enormous eyes swiveled toward him.

Algie sat up. "I'd like to buy that octopus," he said.

"I beg your pardon?" said the man in the yachting cap, as the safari-helmeted man barked "What?"

Algie pursued the advantage of surprise. "I was saving for a microscope, but I'd like that octopus instead. If it wouldn't be too much trouble, sir."

"It certainly would," the man growled. "I have a gentleman's quarrel with this animal."

With a heroic effort, Algie swallowed the opinion that gentlemen did not quarrel with animals. He had to get on this man's good side.

"Algie!" screamed a woman's voice. "Everett! Are you drowned?" In the gathering crowd aboard the steamer, Mrs. Emsworth hurled herself against the rail and flung out her arms, as if she could reach her sons across the separating yards of water.

"We're fine, Mother!" Everett scowled and hunched his shoulders. "Drop it," he growled at Algie. "You're making a spectacle out of us."

"Whiskers off the starboard bow!" cried the second man. "Ransom, I've sighted your sideburn!"

"Keep your voice down!" The other man glared at the snickering crowd and tilted his safari helmet to hide his naked cheek. "Where's that net?"

Algie edged toward the octopus as the man turned away, but the rocking boat betrayed him. The man called Ransom looked over his shoulder.

"I told you, this octopus is not for sale." Taking up the picnic basket, he popped the octopus inside and snapped shut the latch.

"I've almost got it," the man in the yachting cap called. He leaned over the gunnel, reaching for the sideburn with a fishing gaff. "Just a bit closer!"

As the gaff neared its goal, a manatee surfaced beside the boat. Lifting its prehensile lip, it gathered the bobbing whiskers into its mouth and consumed them with a crunch.

17

There was a horrified silence. A few contented bubbles floated up around the manatee's tail.

Then Algie acted—at least, his body did. Without input from his brain, his hands seized the gaff and hooked it around the whiskered man's ankle. Planting his feet, Algie swung his shoulders and body-slammed the man in the solar plexus.

The man shouted, teetering. Algie yanked on the gaff as hard as he could. Everett grabbed for the man's elbow, but it was too late.

"Algie!" his mother shrieked. "What are you doing? Stop that this instant!"

The whiskered man's arms pinwheeled. His boots flew up, and he flipped over the side. The picnic basket bounced in the bottom of the boat. Algie threw it open, snatched the octopus, and flung it overboard.

But the octopus would not fling. It clutched Algie's wrist with all eight arms, and no amount of shaking could pry it loose. Its expression was unmistakable—on no account was it getting back in that water.

The man in the yachting cap was turning around. Algie crammed the octopus into his soaked knapsack.

"Let me aboard," the sideburned man spluttered. "I'm going to strangle that brat!"

"You know the rules," said the man in the yachting cap. "No strangling the guests. Bad for business." To Algie, he whispered, "You shouldn't have done that. He can be unreasonable when he's angry."

Algie smiled apologetically and turned to hide his squirming knapsack.

"I'll ruin you, Aloysius!" the man in the water shouted. "If the newspapers knew half what I could tell—"

"Patience," soothed the man in the yachting cap. "Let me drop these boys off at the pier and greet my guests. They've lowered the gangplank."

Passengers began to file off the steamer. Propelling the boat to the pier with a few strokes, the man sprang up the ladder as the first guest's boots touched the planking. He doffed his yachting cap with as much composure as though he were clad in spotless eveningwear instead of a red-and-white-striped bathing suit.

"Welcome to the Hotel Paraíso," he said. "I am Aloysius Davenport, your humble proprietor."

CHAPTER

3

ALGIE MISSED A step climbing from the skiff to the ladder. He grabbed a rung to keep from falling. So that was Mr. Davenport—capitalist, millionaire, notable eccentric. With the construction of the Hotel Paraíso, he had single-handedly started the luxury resort craze that had swept Florida.

"ALOYSIUS!"

A sickle-shaped fin sliced through the water, headed for the floundering sideburned man.

Mr. Davenport sprang from the pier and landed in the fishing skiff, seized the picnic basket, and sent it spinning over the waves. It hit the water with a *sploosh*. The fin swerved, and the basket vanished in a swirl of gums and teeth.

Algie's heart pounded. He had read about sharks, but no book had prepared him for the lethal agility of that submerged shadow.

The whiskered man swam to the skiff, climbed inside, and bent to slap water from his trousers.

"I told you not to let people feed that creature. It's getting far too aggressive." He sounded annoyed rather than angry, as if hair-raising escapes were only worth a fuss if they made him late for lunch.

Mr. Davenport pointed to a sign on the pier. It read:

FEEDING OF SHARKS, SNAKES, ALLIGATORS, PANTHERS, BOARS, BEARS, BOBCATS, SQUIRRELS, AND ALL OTHER WILDLIFE IS ABSOLUTELY PROHIBITED.

"They don't listen to me," he said. "I wish they would. Strangled guests are bad for business, but eaten ones are worse."

Fortunately for the hotel's reputation, most people had not noticed the shark's murky form in the bustle of disembarking. The whiskered man did not join the crowd but took his oars and rowed off. Mr. Davenport reascended the swim ladder and led the way down the two-hundred foot pier.

Algie raised his eyebrows at Everett, but his brother did not return the look. Everett disappeared into the stream of passengers without a backward glance. Clearly he'd had enough family time for one day.

Beneath the tread of so many boots and shoes, the boardwalk rumbled like a bongo drum. Seagulls wheeled overhead, eyeing the stuffed birds in the ladies' hats.

"Are you all right?" Algie whispered to his knapsack. The octopus wiggled.

"Algie!" Mrs. Emsworth elbowed through her fellow passengers and threw her arms around her son's neck. "I *knew* one of you boys would fall overboard before we were safely ashore! And fighting with a fisherman? You're overexcited . . . if only you'd stayed quietly in your stateroom like I told you!"

"I didn't fall. I was . . . collecting a specimen." Algie wriggled out of his mother's too-affectionate chokehold.

Mrs. Emsworth seized his wrists. "You're bleeding!"

Algie looked down. The barnacled ladder had scratched his palms. Pink trickles mingled with the seawater dripping down his arms.

Ignoring the flow of pedestrians, Mrs. Emsworth knelt in the middle of the boardwalk and pulled out a bucket-size handbag. "I have iodine in here somewhere . . . and gauze, and bandages . . ."

"I'm fine, Mother," Algie said.

"Aha!" Mrs. Emsworth brandished the iodine. Turning Algie's palms upward, she poised the medicine over the torn skin. Her hand wobbled.

"Gracious," she said. "It's the oddest thing, but I . . . I feel rather faint . . . " She swayed.

Algie knew what to do. His mother always reacted this way at the sight of blood.

"Take deep breaths, Mother," he reminded her. Blinking, Mrs. Emsworth put a hand to her head as Algie rummaged in her handbag for the cut-glass vial of smelling salts.

"Thank you, darling." She took a whiff of the vial and grimaced. "How very bracing."

"What's all this?" Lord and Lady Plumworthy had arrived on the scene, mopping their brows in the afternoon sunshine. Good friends of Mrs. Emsworth, they had wintered in Florida for the past two years. It was on their recommendation that Mrs. Emsworth had selected the Hotel Paraíso.

"A dizzy spell, but I'm steadier now." Mrs. Emsworth straightened her hat. "It must be the heat."

Algie was careful to keep his bloody palms out of sight.

A deep-water boathouse beside the dock caught his attention. Inside, a three-masted sailing ship towered over a forest of yachts. Shining gold letters across the stern proclaimed its name: *The Spangled Siren.* A strange symbol gleamed on the hull.

"How peculiar." Lady Plumworthy put up her eyeglasses.

"What do you think that symbol means?" Algie asked. "It looks like two *M*s on top of each other. But with that line through the middle, it could also be two *A*s."

"I don't see any symbol." Lady Plumworthy peered over the crowd. "It looks like straw and taffeta to me. And what seems to be an entire stuffed peacock."

"What are you talking about?"

"Mrs. Pliskett's new hat. It doesn't suit her at all."

At the end of the pier, a tram waited on a wooden platform beside a river opening out of thick, green swamp. Everett hunched in the leading tramcar with Mr. Davenport. He glowered as Algie, Mrs. Emsworth, and the Plumworthies joined them. Mrs. Pliskett squeezed in at the last minute and settled beside Algie with a book.

Mr. Davenport pulled a lever. The tram started off with a rattle and a hiss.

The ocean's blaze vanished as they left the beach and shuddered through shadowy mangrove swamp. Twisted roots thrust upward from the mud, and tiny crabs crept backward, holding their claws en garde. Moss-hung branches squeaked and wailed against the tram's metal sides.

Algie pressed his forehead against the glass. They were crossing yet another stream. White flowers floated down a bayou the color of black tea, twisting and meandering beneath the raised tramway. A brackish, rotting smell filled the air, along with the earthy perfume of a hundred thousand growing things.

By this time the harsh sunlight had dimmed to gloom, and it wasn't all the work of the swamp. What sky showed through the heavy green-and-gray drapery of the tree branches had turned to solid cloud. The scenery reminded Algie of his favorite poem, "The Jabberwocky," about a mysterious wood and a monster.

> *And as in uffish thought he stood,*
> *The Jabberwock, with eyes of flame,*
> *Came whiffling through the tulgey wood,*
> *And burbled as it came.*

As the verses thrummed through Algie's mind, a booming cough echoed between the trees. It didn't sound like thunder. But what creature could make a noise like that?

Mrs. Emsworth peeked out the window, then looked away from the dark swamp with a shudder.

"What are you reading?" she asked Mrs. Pliskett. She tilted her head to see the book's title. "*The Horrible Haunting of Haleyford Hall* by Godric Featheringstone III. Is it any good?"

"You mean you haven't read it?" Mrs. Pliskett raised bejeweled fingers in astonishment.

"No. Should I have?" Mrs. Emsworth's cheeks flushed, and Algie remembered her worries over appearing behind-the-times at this stylish resort.

"My dear," said Mrs. Pliskett, "you must be the only one in the nation who hasn't."

"What's it about?" Algie asked.

Mrs. Pliskett dropped her rich, throaty voice. "A group of guests in an isolated manor house—"

"STOP!" Lord and Lady Plumworthy shouted.

"We're halfway through." Lady Plumworthy lifted a copy from her handbag. "Such bone-chilling suspense!"

"If you think that work of fiction is frightening," said Mrs. Pliskett, "I should make you aware of recent happenings *at this very hotel*!" She brandished a newspaper, and Mrs. Emsworth jumped.

"H—happenings?" she quavered.

Lady Plumworthy patted Mrs. Emsworth's hand. "Don't worry, dear. The truth in these gossip papers wouldn't fill a thimble." To Mrs. Pliskett she said, "Caroline, you may fill us in *after* we're snug with a nice cup of tea at the hotel."

The paper's headline read: "MYSTERY AT THE HOTEL PARAÍSO."

"May I read that?" Algie asked. Mrs. Pliskett passed it over. The newspaper was a Florida society report, *The Tittle-Tattle*. Beneath a list of guests registered at the Hotel Paraíso came the article in question.

> *"Only a week into its season, disturbing tales haunt the Hotel Paraíso. Distinguished performer Madam Maximus claims to have been attacked while bathing in the resort's famous mineral spring.*
>
> *"'I was enjoying the waters at dawn,' the athletic entertainer explained, 'when something seized my ankle. Like a hand, but larger and stronger than any human's.'*
>
> *"Madam Maximus states she was jerked beneath the water and would have drowned if the 'hand' had not released her with enough breath to surface. At the time of printing, no hotel staff were available for comment. Owner Aloysius Davenport offered this statement: 'Poppycock.'"*

Algie lifted his eyes and saw Mr. Davenport staring out the window, jolting with the movement of the tram.

> *"The alarming incident,"* the article continued, *"occurred during an ongoing mystery plague killing off sea life at the Paraíso's beaches. In addition to doubt cast over the wholesomeness of the resort's air, increased public attention has brought to light a ghoulish detail. According to local legend, the hotel is constructed on*

26

the site of an eighteenth-century Spanish ruin abandoned after the disappearance of its owner. While it remains to be seen whether visitors are deterred by these unsettling circumstances, speculation has risen that the hotel is cursed."

"Strange, is it not?" said Mrs. Pliskett to Algie in a low voice. "A lonely mansion, a mysterious plague . . . "

"You don't really believe the hotel is cursed?" Algie handed the newspaper back.

"Why not?" Mrs. Pliskett shook her head. On her hat, the stuffed peacock's glass eyes stared into the distance. "It was Shakespeare who said 'There are more things in heaven and earth, Horatio, than are dreamt of in your philosophy.'"

Chills crawled up the back of Algie's neck. The booming cough echoed through the swamp again.

"Do you have banshees, Mr. Davenport?" Mrs. Pliskett asked, raising her voice. "Perhaps with head colds?"

"Bull alligators," said Mr. Davenport. Then he yanked the tram brake as hard as he could. The vehicle dug in its heels and stopped inches from disaster.

CHAPTER

4

THE WOODEN TRAMWAY had been ripped apart. A fifteen-foot section of planking had vanished, the edges of polished boards showing raw and splintered. The torn-away planking was nowhere to be seen. There was no sign of it in the bayou, the undergrowth, or even the treetops.

Mr. Davenport rubbed his jaw. "Must have been a small tornado. Our weather can be unpredictable."

As he spoke, a flash of lightning seared across the sky, followed by a thunderclap that rattled the windows. The trees tossed their heads.

Then the rain hit. One minute they were snug and secure in their brass-and-plate-glass tramcar, and the next they were smacked by a splatter of rain so heavy it sounded like golf balls on the roof. The downpour battered their ears and slid past the panes in sheets. Soon the windows fogged over with the anxious breath of the guests.

Algie rubbed a circle with his sleeve, but all he could see was sliding rain on a blurry greenish background. The circle fogged over again. Trapped in the hot carriage, unable to see out, Algie felt claustrophobic and breathless. He remembered his mysterious sighting in the ocean. What if he wiped the glass again and that yellow eye stared in at him?

SPLAT! Something slapped the window by his face.

Algie yelled and fell backward onto the floor. A pale, sprawling, four-fingered hand was plastered against the glass!

Mrs. Emsworth screamed.

"It's all right." Lord Plumworthy wiped the glass clear.

The "hand" gathered itself together and clambered up the windowpane. What Algie had mistaken for disjointed fingers were actually the legs of a tree frog.

"Sorry." Algie's cheeks felt sunburned. Everett pried him off the floor in silence.

"How," said Lady Plumworthy, speaking everyone's thought, "exactly, are we to continue without an intact tramway?"

"I'll hike for help," said Mr. Davenport. "It shouldn't take long."

"I'll go too." Algie brushed himself off. The hot, closed-in tram car was stifling. He needed fresh air.

"Certainly NOT, you won't," said Mrs. Emsworth. "I won't have you wandering the storm with crocodiles and leopards and goodness knows what else."

Algie tried to protest, but the words stuck in his throat. His windpipe constricted. He swallowed twice and squeezed a breath. He was not going to have an asthma attack. Not here. Things were going to be different here. He looked at Everett for support. But Everett had gone back to ignoring Algie, drumming his fingers on the windowsill.

"Let him go," Lord Plumworthy said. "Do the boy good to run out some energy after being cooped up on a boat."

"Yes," Mrs. Pliskett intoned, "much better for him to be away from the herd. So many auras close together has the propensity to draw—" she looked around, and dropped her voice, "—well, perhaps it would be best not to say."

To Algie's surprise, democracy won the day. The doors opened, and he and Mr. Davenport stepped out into the rain.

As Mr. Davenport climbed gingerly off the broken edge of boardwalk and scanned for a way to ascend the other side, Algie took a moment to check on his octopus. How long could it survive out of water? The canvas bag was soaking wet, which Algie hoped would help keep the animal comfortable. Still, it needed water at some point. Perhaps the hotel had a fish tank where he could hide it while figuring out what to do . . . He thought of the dead sea creatures on the beach. Would the octopus die if he returned it to the ocean?

Algie lifted the flap of his knapsack. Wide, innocent eyes stared up at him.

"What are you—? Hey!" Algie hissed at the octopus. "That's my compass!"

The octopus waved the compass arrow with one arm. The instrument's dial, glass face, and other components were scattered about the bag.

Algie attempted to pry the arrow away. The octopus hung on, swatting him with several arms.

"Over here!" Mr. Davenport called. He shimmied up a tree and stepped from its crook onto the elevated tramway. "Best foot forward!"

Algie gave up and closed the bag. The tree ascent was a scramble, but he managed it with Mr. Davenport's help. They set off down the boardwalk.

"Stay with me and don't wander off the tramway," Mr. Davenport said. "Just as a precaution—there's not much that can harm you in this swamp, unless you step in an alligator nest or run afoul of a cottonmouth. Bears won't usually bother you unless you bother them. We don't have many venomous spiders. Stay away from wild pigs, though."

Algie nodded. If Mr. Davenport kept reassuring him, he wasn't certain he'd have the courage to continue.

After fifteen minutes passed without wild beasts descending on him, Algie began to relax. The rain slowed to a patter. Warm, humid air loosened the tightness in his chest. He tromped along, enjoying the hollow shudder of the tramway underfoot.

The mist was so dense that they almost walked off the second damaged area before seeing it. This time, lightning had split a great cypress in half. Both pieces had toppled onto the tramway and destroyed a significant portion. Standing at the edge of the gap, Algie tried not to imagine what it would have looked like if lightning had struck the tram instead.

"Don't go any farther." Mr. Davenport laid a hand on Algie's arm as the broken tramway swayed. "We'll have to climb down and around again."

This time, the process was more difficult. The boardwalk stood higher off the ground in this section, and it was a six-foot drop into leaf mulch. Tangled, waist-high undergrowth made progress almost impossible, and they had to detour a long way around. Sweat glistened on Algie's nose when he crossed his eyes. His arms were dotted with mosquitoes. Ducking beneath a thorny vine, he pushed through a barrier of cobwebs and stopped.

An ankle-deep stream barred the way, emerging from a dark tunnel of trees. Bathtub-clear, the water neither chattered nor rippled but lay silent and still between its banks. To the right, slices of light through the trees suggested the main river close by.

Algie splashed through the water, keeping an eye out for cottonmouths. On the far side, he turned.

Mr. Davenport was nowhere in sight.

CHAPTER

5

"DON'T PANIC," ALGIE said, louder than he meant to. Professor Champion had not panicked in *Peregrinations Through Peru,* when he'd noticed the log on which he was fording a piranha-laced river was no log at all, but a massive caiman. The current situation was not nearly so dire.

Of course, Professor Champion had not been twelve years old at the time, or wandering a cursed hotel ground. It did seem like bad luck. Five minutes off the tramway and Algie was minus one adult, stranded alone in a dense wood that looked every minute more likely to have something come whiffling through it. Maybe Mr. Davenport had strolled down to the river to get his bearings.

Or maybe a swamp monster had clutched him by the ankle and dragged him down into muck. Maybe banshees had been drawn to his lone aura. Maybe bull alligators had. Algie's legs went tingly. His head swam. His heartbeat whooshed in his ears.

Branches crackled upstream, away from the light of the river.

"Mr. Davenport?" Algie called.

The crackling stopped.

Algie's knapsack began to thrash. He had almost forgotten the octopus. Frightened that it might be smothering, he unbuckled his bag and took it out.

The octopus had lost interest in the compass and was now a vibrant pink. Holding it to his chest, Algie tiptoed upstream in the direction of the noise. At the bend in the stream, he glanced over his shoulder. He could barely see the tramway through the fog.

Algie straightened his shoulders. Good posture might give him courage. He took one more step and peered around a clump of ferns.

At first, he thought he was standing on the edge of a bottomless hole. But no, it was a spring, filled with water so clear that Algie had to look twice. A dark fissure in the center twisted downward out of sight, writhing away into the earth. Moss-covered stones the size of footballs dotted the streambed by his feet.

He lifted his eyes, and a tingling shock raced through him.

On the near bank, a hairy gray-black lump bulged from the crook of a tree. The lump looked like a huge squirrels' nest—if squirrels' nests had tusks and long, mean snouts. It was a wild boar, wedged upside down in the branches.

Algie's stomach lurched. Who would stuff a dead pig in a tree? The gray light seemed to dim.

Dead leaves crackled again. Algie heard a loud *thump* and slither of something heavy sliding over sandy soil. Bamboo wavered and shook, but there was no wind. Something—something huge and alive—was lurking behind it.

The octopus in Algie's arms exploded into motion. Terrified, Algie stepped backward and tripped over one of the mossy rocks. He dropped the octopus as he fell. It hit the water and zipped into the spring. Algie's umbrella hat tipped over his eyes. He crawled blindly forward, knelt on the mosquito net, and yanked the hat off.

The stream was turning black. Clouds of darkness bloomed in the water, spreading and reaching for him with inky tendrils. Algie splashed backward away from them. The black water crept forward and swirled around him. His socks turned gray.

High in the branches, the boar's eyes flew open. With a squealing heave, it wrested itself free and thudded to the ground. It staggered upright, flicking its ears and shuddering. Its beady eyes landed on Algie.

Algie bounced to his feet and sprinted for the nearest tree. He leaped up the base, climbing the network of roots.

The pig charged. Algie pulled himself higher as sharp hooves scrabbled at the trunk just below.

Panting, Algie wedged his elbow between two vines. His arms shook. If he reached the tree's crown, he could rest. He tried to step again, and his boot jammed in a crack.

Algie tugged. He was stuck fast. His arms weren't strong enough to hold on much longer. If he couldn't reach a better perch, he would lose his grip and fall—right onto the boar's razor-sharp tusks.

Voices floated over the swamp, coming from the tramway. Two white forms glimmered through the mist.

Algie gathered his courage. He would take ghosts over boars any day.

"Help!" he cried.

The white figures came on. Any minute, his arms would fail. Desperate, Algie jerked his foot as hard as he could. The boot popped free, and Algie lost his grip. He slithered down the trunk and landed on the boar's back.

CHAPTER

6

FOR A MINUTE it was difficult to tell who was more startled — Algie or the boar. Then the boar snorted and ran. It shot under the tramway, and Algie ducked. Miraculously, he kept his seat.

"It's getting away!" one of the ghosts shouted.

A snakelike object whizzed through the air and settled around Algie's shoulders. It yanked him off into the mud. He kicked and struggled as he was hauled backward and hoisted onto the tramway.

Two girls in white dresses stood over him. The smaller girl held two umbrellas. The older girl's hands were occupied with landing Algie, which she had accomplished by slinging her lasso over a tree branch for leverage.

"Why were you harassing that boar?" She set a boot on Algie's chest, pushing him into the tram tracks.

"I wasn't." Algie spat mud. "Not on purpose."

"You could have gotten your guts gouged out. Or worse, hurt the pig." The girl dug her heel into his solar plexus.

"He couldn't have hurt the pig," said the younger girl. "He isn't big enough. Let him up."

Claws pricked Algie's skin as a heavy weight climbed onto his chest. A bird with a lizard-like head peered into his face with long-lashed brown eyes.

The older girl withdrew her foot and began to coil her rope.

"He's not for eating," she said.

"Definitely not." Algie sat up carefully, so the bird had time to climb down.

"I was talking to Hamlet. He's a *Cathartes aura*."

"A turkey vulture," said the shorter girl. "Don't worry. He wouldn't eat you even if you were dead. He likes sirloin."

"A vulture," said Algie, swallowing. "Named Hamlet."

"Because he's always brooding," said the lasso girl. "He broke his wing when he was a baby. It didn't heal right, so we had to keep him. Are you Algie Emsworth?"

"How did you know?"

"I'm Francisca Davenport and this is my sister Lourdes. We saw Papa in the swamp a few minutes ago, chasing a butterfly for his collection. He asked us to find you and bring you back to the hotel."

"He left me in the middle of the swamp for a butterfly?"

Unsure whether to be offended or impressed, Algie accepted Francisca's hand. She pulled him to his feet with ease. Her palm was rough and calloused.

"Don't take it personally." Lourdes lifted Hamlet to her shoulder. "Papa's always like that. Whenever he sees something he wants, it knocks everything else out of his head."

They set off down the tramway. Algie fell into step beside the girls, stretching his pace to match theirs. Francisca was taller than he, but seemed around his own age. She had long blondeish hair bleached lighter by sun, and a crooked nose. Lourdes looked a year or two younger, with brown eyes, curly brown hair, and pointed eyebrows. One of her cheeks dimpled as she smiled.

"There's never any guests our own age," she said. "They're at boarding or finishing school during the hotel season. Papa used to keep us in school, too, but we always managed to get expelled before Christmas. Now he knows it's easier to let us take a vacation during the season."

Algie blinked, unsure how to respond.

"Have you lived in Florida your whole lives?" he asked.

"All the best parts," Lourdes said. "So, what are you, anyway?"

"Um," Algie said, "*Homo sapiens*, to the best of my knowledge."

"No," said Francisca. "She means, what are you when you don't have to be anything else? We're both field biologists."

"Not real ones," Lourdes said. "We haven't gotten anything published yet."

"That doesn't mean we're phonies," said Francisca. "They'll publish us sooner or later."

"That's like me!" Algie exclaimed. "I'm a naturalist and an explorer."

"Mira sus brazos," Francisca remarked to Lourdes. "Un caracol es más musculoso que este chico."

Algie looked from her to Lourdes.

"Don't be horrible, Frankie," said Lourdes. To Algie she explained, "Frankie thinks it's big to speak Spanish when other people can't understand."

Francisca crossed her eyes at Lourdes.

"Are you from Spain?" Algie asked.

"No," Lourdes said. "We're American. But Papa's mother was from Cuba, and so was our mama. Frankie was born in Cuba, but then Mama and Papa moved to Florida because of the fighting with Spain."

Algie nodded. "So that's why your first names sound Spanish, but not your last?"

"That's right," Lourdes said. "My real name's María de Lourdes, but you can call me Lulu."

"And you go by Frankie?" Algie asked Francisca.

"Not to you," she said.

Lulu huffed.

Halting, Frankie crossed her arms, planted her feet, and scanned Algie from his boots to his umbrella hat. All at once he was uncomfortably aware of his skinny arms and schoolboy trousers.

"Where did you say you're from?" she asked.

"Chicago." Algie put his hands in his pockets to hide their lack of calluses.

40

"What's an eft?" was the next question Frankie fired at him.

"That's easy," Algie said. "The terrestrial juvenile phase of a newt."

"How would you classify a worm lizard? Is it a worm, or a lizard?"

"Trick question," Algie said. "Neither. Worm lizards belong to the family Amphisbaenidae."

"You've got book learning." Frankie looked impressed. "But it takes more than that to be a biologist in Florida. What's an easy way to get a bat out of a parlor full of screaming tourists?"

"I don't know," Algie said. "Maybe you could teach me while I'm here?"

"Trick question. There is no easy way." Frankie grinned, then grew serious again. "Listen, city slicker. If you're going to hang around with us, you'll have to keep up. Got it? The hotel season is only so long, we've got a lot of fieldwork to get done, and we don't slow down for anyone."

"Got it," Algie said. He resolved not to let Frankie's attitude bother him. He was a city slicker, and these sisters were obviously masters of swampcraft. If he was going to learn from them, they'd have to get along.

"So," Frankie asked as they resumed their walk, "why were you racing a boar through the swamp?"

A shiver shook Algie's stomach as he recalled the afternoon's events. Would the girls believe him if he told?

The tramline ended and the trees opened up.

CHAPTER

7

GREEN . . . SO MUCH GREEN. Algie had never seen anything as green as that grass.

An enormous lake lapped the edges of the lawn, its boundaries lost in swamp. Marching up from the water, a double rank of topiary animals flanked a gravel walk that swept toward what looked like a Spanish castle complete with domes, towers, and archways. Surrounded by wilderness, the grand hotel should have looked out of place. But it didn't. Its vivid tiles mirrored the blue lake, green mangroves, and orange-streaked sunset.

Lulu frowned.

"What's wrong with the topiary?" she asked.

As they drew near the leafy sculptures, Algie understood. No matter what shape each bush had begun as—brontosaurus, swan, serpent, rabbit—its outlines were now swollen and deformed. They didn't look like whimsical garden guardians. They looked like an army of gargoyles.

Algie glanced back at the darkening swamp. It was too easy to imagine those misshapen bushes stirring to life in the twilight. Some of the sculptures reached fifteen feet high.

As if picking up on the uneasy mood, Hamlet the vulture hunched and bobbed.

"They haven't been trimmed." Frankie ran her hand across the leaves of a giant hare. "I wonder why?"

"Don't you live here?" Algie was glad to turn his mind to normal questions.

"We just got back from boarding school by riverboat this afternoon," Lulu explained. "Papa doesn't like us to come until after the opening. He says it's too much like having live explosives around the place."

"The first thing we always do is run to the beach, but we had to stop and rescue you instead," Frankie said.

"It wasn't a rescue," said Algie.

"No?" Frankie raised an eyebrow. "Did you have a plan for getting off that pig?"

"Papa will know what's going on," Lulu said. "Maybe the gardeners are sick or on strike." But she looked worried.

As they passed beneath the iron gate, electric lights winked on. They emerged into a garden courtyard festooned with lightbulbs. Potted palms waved across a goldfish pond, and the chatter of fountain water echoed off the stone walls.

In the atrium, Mr. Davenport was briefing a grumpy-looking man holding a ladder under one arm and a lantern in the other.

"The guests are trapped two-thirds of the way down the line," Mr. Davenport said. "You won't get the horse and cart beyond the lightning strike, so they'll have to walk for a stretch. Spin it as a pleasant nature stroll, 'The cry of the night-flying heron,' and that sort of thing, you know."

Frankie pulled Algie onward. "Come on!" she said. "We'll give you the grand tour."

Before long, Algie had lost his bearings in a maze of parlors and passages. Lulu and Frankie each assumed the mantle of tour guide, neither seeming bothered by the necessity of talking over the other.

"—the library is off that hall, but the best natural history books are in the map room—"

"—stay away from the Bird of Paradise Parlor, it's always filled with ladies telling you how precocious you are—"

As they wound deeper into the building, Algie kept expecting to run across staff or other guests. The hallways were deserted. Dust clouded the decorative glass showcases holding seashells and other curiosities. Some of the lightbulbs illuminating the passages had burned out and not been replaced. Beyond the windows, the miles of empty swampland pressed against Algie's consciousness.

A bar of music lilted around the corner.

"I thought so!" Frankie towed Algie up a long staircase. They emerged into a dazzle of lights and voices.

The staircase opened onto a ring-shaped ballroom. Couples in long gowns and tailcoats waltzed past, the ladies' hats waving with plumes.

"Watch out!" Lulu pulled Algie backward as he was almost mowed down by a swirling skirt.

A splash and a burst of applause sounded below. Seizing a gap in the dance, Algie and the girls hurried to the railing in the center of the room. They looked down two stories into an indoor swimming pool. Guests in colorful swimwear splashed in the water or sat in chairs around the perimeter. A small orchestra played from a platform at the far end. One enterprising gentleman had procured a rowboat and was serenading a cargo of ladies.

"800,000 gallons," said Frankie with pride. "It was the biggest pool in America for a long time. What do you think?"

"It's amazing," Algie said. It reminded him of the time his mother had taken him to the opera. This scene, too, seemed larger than life, glittering and protected from the darkness beyond the windows.

All around the walls, lightbulbs flickered and went out. Darkness swallowed the room.

CHAPTER

8

A **CHORUS OF** gasps and several screams rose from the assembly. The band wavered and fell silent.

"I hope I'm not fussy," said a woman near Algie, "but for twenty-five dollars a night, I *do* like to see where I'm going." A hum of complaints buzzed throughout the hall.

Beside Algie a beam of light cut the darkness. Frankie brandished a brass-capped cylinder.

"Electric flashlight," she explained, answering Algie's astonishment. "Papa gave it to me last Christmas. They're not commercially available."

"Miss Frankie, Miss Lulu—I see you're back." A red-bearded man swooped down on the trio and snatched Frankie's flashlight. "I need to borrow this."

"That's O'Conner, the manager," Lulu whispered to Algie.

"You're welcome," Frankie grumbled, as O'Conner waved the light at the guests.

"A temporary power outage," he called. "No doubt some wires knocked loose by the rain. If all guests will remain in place, staff will be around shortly to escort everyone to their rooms."

As Algie's eyes grew used to the darkness, the alcove windows at the sides of the ballroom shimmered blue with starlight. He sidled toward them. Other guests gravitated to the glow as well.

"It reminds me of a scene from that book," said one dancer. "*The Horrible Haunting of Haleyford Hall*. Remember the chapter where the gaslights go out, and they find—"

"Don't!" said her partner. "I remember. What do you think of this 'curse' on the hotel? Did you hear Madam Maximus's story?"

"From her own mouth," said the girl. "*I* want to know more about this legend of the Spaniard who disappeared in the lake."

Frankie snorted. "It's a 'legend' now? That's the first I've heard of it." The couple turned to stare at her.

"Frankie," Lulu whispered.

"Sorry," Frankie said. She did not sound apologetic.

Algie leaned against the window. On this side of the hotel, a glass greenhouse overlooked the lawn. The lake curved past in a gentle crescent, serene beneath the stars.

Except . . . except something was not serene. A shadow crept across the grass, shambling toward the lake. Huge and blobby, it looked like one of the topiary animals gone rogue, abandoning its post.

Algie's head whirled. He reached for Lulu and clutched Hamlet instead. The vulture retaliated with a sharp peck.

"Ouch!"

"Hamlet!" Lulu scolded.

"Look!" Holding his stinging wrist, Algie pointed.

Frankie and Lulu crowded to the window.

"What?" Frankie asked.

Algie scanned the grounds, but the hulking shape was gone. He remembered the eye in the ocean and shivered. What was going on? He took a deep breath and turned to the girls.

Frankie and Lulu listened without interrupting as Algie told the story of the afternoon. The yellow eye, the newspaper article, the boar in the tree, and the unseen slithering thing . . . the only point he left out was his asthma.

"It reminds me of alligators," Frankie said, after Algie recounted the boar's mysterious revival. "Sometimes they'll wedge their kills between roots or under bridges and come back for it. But no gator could stuff a pig six feet up a tree."

"Let's go back to our rooms." Lulu sounded upset.

"We should show Algie to his room first," Frankie said. "But we have to find out which it is."

Careful in the darkness, they circled the ballroom. Guests leaned in alcoves, chattering or complaining, while candles appeared, marking staff members lighting people back to their rooms. Each was surrounded by such a crush of guests that it was impossible to get anyone's attention.

"There's Papa!" Frankie stepped forward and stopped. "Hold on—he's always in a bad mood when he's with O'Conner."

Mr. Davenport and the red-bearded manager stood by the railing. O'Conner held the flashlight pointed at the ground.

"—recovered my guests from the swamp yet?" Mr. Davenport whispered.

"They arrived a few minutes ago," O'Conner soothed. "A little disheveled, but none the worse for wear."

"Much good that will do us, if we can't hold a simple dance without losing power." Mr. Davenport rubbed his neck. "This isn't going to help with that rigmarole about a curse."

O'Conner pursed his lips, tapping the flashlight against his thigh.

"When you fire most of the staff," he said at last, "including gardeners and electricians, there are bound to be incidents—"

Mr. Davenport sighed. "Yes, but I don't know how else to cut costs. This place has been draining my wallet for two years, and we've already lost more guests than I can afford. If we can't put an end to these rumors, I'll have no choice but to close the hotel."

Algie's stomach plummeted. Frankie and Lulu gasped.

"In the middle of the season?" O'Conner's voice echoed the children's shock.

"Yes," said Mr. Davenport. "If it doesn't pay, it goes."

CHAPTER

9

"**MAYBE THIS PLACE** won't be so bad," Everett remarked the next morning, as a lime-green butterfly flitted past his nose.

Algie waited until Everett was looking the other way and then fished a caterpillar out of his brother's teacup. He patted it dry with a napkin and transferred it to a potted fern.

The breakfast room doubled as a solarium for Mr. Davenport's live butterfly collection. Swallowtails and monarchs filled the air, along with the tinkle of silverware. Two tables over, a hummingbird whizzed in and out of the artificial flowers on Mrs. Pliskett's hat.

"Are you feeling well, Algie?" Mrs. Emsworth examined his plate. "You haven't eaten much."

"I'm all right," Algie said. It wasn't true. His stomach was heavy with worry over what he had heard the night before. If the hotel went belly-up, so did Algie's dreams of scientific discovery. He'd be right back to staring at sad zoo animals or stalking the squirrels in Lincoln Park.

"I'll take you to soak in the mineral springs after breakfast." Mrs. Emsworth straightened Algie's collar. "I hope you didn't catch yellow fever in that swamp. Afterward, you'll need a nap—"

"Did you know, Mother, I heard Mrs. Pliskett say she and Lady Plumworthy are taking a glass-bottom boat tour this morning?" Everett interrupted. "They didn't mention it, because they know you're frightened of alligators."

"Me? Frightened? Why, I sat up till two o'clock with that Haleyford book last night and didn't turn a hair!" Mrs. Emsworth bristled. "I'm sure I could brave an alligator as well as Caroline Pliskett."

"I'm only repeating what I heard," Everett said. "May I take Algie to the pool?"

Mrs. Emsworth hesitated.

"Algie can't swim," she said. "And he's so delicate."

"Mother," Algie groaned. Much as he loved his mother, her hovering drove him wild.

"If you keep fussing over him, he'll stay that way," said Everett. "Remember the doctor's orders. If you want Algie's lungs to get stronger, he needs fresh air and exercise. Isn't that why we're here?"

Algie's heart bounced with Everett's support. He imagined long hikes and boat rides together, Everett teaching him older-brotherly things like how to bait hooks and goalkeep.

"I want to go with Everett," he said.

"I'll teach him to swim," Everett said. "And I'll make sure he stays out of trouble."

"If you're sure . . ." Mrs. Emsworth glanced at the Plumworthies rising from their table. "I don't think I'd mind seeing an alligator—from a nice, seaworthy boat, of course. It sounds rather . . . thrilling!" She took a fan from her bag and wafted air against her cheeks. It was the first time Algie had seen her look excited about anything since their father died.

"Are you really going to teach me to swim?" Algie demanded, once their mother was out of earshot.

"Why not? Mother needs a holiday as much as you do. Something to interest her besides imagining smallpox into every mosquito bite." Everett twisted in his seat. "What's going on over there?"

A murmur rose on the far side of the solarium. People stood to peer through the high French doors opening onto the garden.

Algie and Everett hurried over. Twelve feet above the lawn, a young woman with red-gold hair strolled a high wire between two coconut palms. She hooked her parasol over one shoulder and drew her elbows behind her head, stretching her shoulders.

Algie turned to Everett, but he was no longer there. A crowd of onlookers had spilled outside and was applauding on the lawn. Everett stood among them.

A freckled young man leaned against the doorframe near Algie. A copy of *The Horrible Haunting of Haleyford Hall* by Godric Featheringstone III was tucked under his arm.

"Who's that?" Algie pointed to the wire walker.

"I can tell you're not from around here." The young man half-smiled. "Angel O'Dare is a Southern celebrity. She's the lead performer for Madam Maximus and the Aerial Acrobats."

Overhead, Angel O'Dare bounced twice and did a front flip.

"The whole troupe is wintering at the hotel," said the man. "They're giving a performance in the pool hall tonight."

Angel O'Dare jumped and spun. Just as it seemed she would plummet to the ground, she caught the wire with her parasol handle. The crowd gasped.

Everett stepped forward and Angel dropped into his arms. Alarm bells exploded in Algie's head. *Emergency!* Once Everett got distracted, there was no telling what or who he might back out on. Then it would be goodbye swimming lessons.

"I have to go!" Algie hopped in distress. "Have a good day, Mr.—"

"James," said the man. "Parker James."

Wriggling through skirts and tweedy legs, Algie came out beneath the high wire.

"Ah, Algie," said Everett, spotting him. He wore his most annoying grown-up expression. "Miss O'Dare, this is my little brother. I can't play right now, Algie. Miss O'Dare and I are engaged for singles tennis."

"You're engaged to teach me to swim." Algie planted his feet.

"We'll go later." Everett scowled.

Algie knew the symptoms. Everett would be good for nothing after a morning spent with Angel. The throes of love and rejection were equally all-consuming and boring in Algie's experience—at least if the subject was sixteen and Everett. Algie did not want to listen to "Miss O'Dare" this and "Miss O'Dare" that all afternoon.

"You promised me first." He looked at Angel. If she were the right sort, she wouldn't stand for it.

"Be a good kid, and I'll show you how to turn a cartwheel sometime." Angel dusted her hands on her athletic bloomers. "Mr. Emsworth—" turning to Everett, "—thanks so much for inviting me to tennis. I wouldn't have an excuse to avoid Mr. James otherwise, and he's getting stickier than a blob of pine sap."

She moved off, Everett bobbing beside her. Her arms looked muscular. Despite the harsh sun, she was barely sweating.

Algie hoped she would destroy Everett at tennis.

CHAPTER

10

FRANKIE AND LULU, dressed in matching blue-and-white bathing suits, hurried down the gravel drive toward the river.

"Algie!" Lulu waved.

The tightness in Algie's chest lifted. Some people wanted him around, even if Everett didn't.

"Are you going swimming?" he asked, joining them.

"We're launching a research expedition," Lulu said. "Do you want to come?"

"Lulu!" Frankie glared at her. Algie's ribs contracted at her belligerent tone.

"What?" Lulu said. "He could join the FLEAS. We need new blood."

"What's a FLEA?" Algie pretended not to notice Frankie's huff.

"The Floridian Lady Explorers and Scientists," Lulu said. "Frankie and I are the only members right now."

"I don't think I meet the qualifications," Algie said.

"We could change the name. The Floridian Legendary Explorers and Scientists."

"That doesn't describe me either."

"Not yet." Lulu nudged her sister. "Frankie, come on."

"I don't want to get in the way," Algie said, though he was longing to join. "And I don't mind not being a FLEA. I mean a FLEAS."

Frankie studied him. Lulu linked her arm through Algie's.

"Fine," Frankie said. "But if you're joining our crew, remember I'm the captain."

"Where are we going?" Algie asked.

"We'll take some observations by the ocean dock, where you saw that eye in the water. If there's something funny going on around here, we need to figure out what."

"Your father wasn't serious yesterday, was he?" Algie asked. "He wouldn't shut down the hotel?"

"Papa is a businessman." Frankie looked grim. "There's not a millionaire on earth with enough money to run this place if it won't pay for part of its own upkeep. Papa won't wait for bankruptcy. He'll close the hotel tomorrow if he thinks it'll cut his losses. We've got to get to the bottom of this fast—before we lose any more guests."

Algie was glad to shake off gloomy thoughts as they entered the boathouse. Ripples of light slid across the high ceiling, and the *slap-slap* of wavelets echoed off the walls. The lakeside boathouse was smaller than the deep-water one that sheltered the yachts and tall ship beside the pier, but it had room for watercraft of every description.

"There she is." Frankie waved an arm. "The FLEAS official research vessel. We refurbished her last year."

The *Diving Belle* was a small barge with a pilothouse for the boat's wheel in front and an odd bell-shaped structure by the stern. Algie looked on in surprise as Frankie placed a handle in a piece of machinery and started cranking.

"What's that?" he asked.

"Petrol engine," Frankie grunted. She jumped back as the motor banged, shuddered, and began to rumble. Smoke poured from its seams.

The *Belle* grumbled down the lake toward the river, heading for the ocean. Algie leaned over the side as the bow pushed through the water. *The bow is the front of the boat, the stern is the back,* he reminded himself. He didn't want to sound like a landlubber. Sunlight pierced the water and sank into greeny-blue nothingness.

"How deep is this lake?" he asked.

"It's actually a headspring," Lulu said. Frankie was in the wheelhouse, leaving her sister to play host. "The Señora's Spring. There are spots so deep they've never found the bottom. Did you bring a swimsuit?"

"In my bag." Algie tried not to sound envious. His knapsack of supplies seemed pitiful compared to the girls' setup. He tugged his umbrella hat over his ears.

"We're hoping to convince Papa to get us a pair of diving suits next season." Lulu ran her finger over the rivets of the *Belle*'s rail. "If there *is* a next season."

"There will be." Algie straightened his shoulders. "Everything will be all right, once we prove the hotel isn't cursed."

"What if it is?" Lulu asked.

"Have you been reading *The Horrible Haunting of Haleyford Hall*?"

Lulu laughed. "Hasn't everyone? But it doesn't make a difference."

"Yes, it does," Algie said. "Everyone is jumpy. There's some natural explanation we're all overlooking."

"What's your explanation for that thing you saw on the lawn last night?"

Algie hesitated. He did not *think* he had been hallucinating. But with his medication, how could he be sure? It was a natural explanation—just not one he wanted to share with Lulu. A good naturalist and explorer should be rugged, invincible. One did not read about Professor Champion puffing on a Carbolic Asthma Ball.

"How does that *Haleyford* book end?" he asked instead of answering. "Is it like a Sherlock Holmes story where you think something supernatural is going on, but in the end it turns out there isn't?"

"Yes," Lulu admitted.

"There you go," Algie said. "I'm sure it'll be like that."

"I hope not," Lulu said. "In the book, Lord Haleyford takes quack medicine to make himself immortal and ends up going insane and trying to murder all his house guests."

"Oh." Algie swallowed. That was not the kind of ending he had in mind. "Why'd he want to be immortal?"

"There was some family illness he didn't want to get. A natural explanation doesn't mean it's not scary."

"You're right," Algie said. "But I'd rather know the truth. Even if it's scary."

"So would I." Lulu shook back her curly hair. "Come on, I'll show you the laboratory."

★

They had reached the river mouth now and were chugging from estuary into open ocean. Most of the barge's rear deck was occupied by the dome-shaped structure Algie had noticed earlier. It resembled a wooden bell jar, dotted with porthole windows.

Algie followed Lulu as she climbed a ladder up the side of the dome and descended through a hatch in the top.

"Why isn't there an ordinary door?" he asked.

"Waterproofing," Lulu said. "You'll see!"

They emerged into a round paneled room. Lockers and fold-down shelves lined the walls, and thick porthole glass lent a green otherworldliness to the light. A square hole in the floor, guarded by a grate, looked down to the ocean's surface.

"Is that so you can observe fish?" Algie peeked through the grate. He took care not to step on it.

"Like I said, you'll see." Lulu unlocked a cupboard, took down a heavy book, and handed it to Algie.

Sketches and watercolors of sea life filled its pages. Algie saw manatees grazing meadows of seagrass, a close-up of the pattern of spots on a pufferfish, a lantern-jawed eel peeping from its hole. Neat cursive handwriting filled the pages opposite the pictures: observations on behavior, feeding, and habitats.

"'The octopus paralyzes its prey with a toxic nip,'" Algie read aloud, and turned another page. "'Pelicans work in tandem with dolphins as they herd fish against the mangroves.'"

"I illustrate, and Frankie writes up the notes." Lulu lifted the lid on an aquarium bolted to the wall, where seahorses knotted their tails around strands of waterweed. Other tanks contained sea cucumbers, anemones, jellyfish, and hermit crabs.

Algie brushed his fingers across a painting of a pod of dolphins pictured from below. Lulu had captured the white ball of sun blurred by the rippling surface. In the mysterious light of the portholes, Chicago's skyscrapers seemed planets away.

He could not let the hotel close and shut him out of this bright place with clear edges where anything could happen. It was his one chance to become a real naturalist.

"Why is it your one chance?" Lulu asked, tilting her head.

"No reason." Algie blushed. He hadn't realized he'd spoken aloud—a habit from spending most of his time alone. Though he told his mother she worried too much, Algie never told anyone how much he himself worried over his doctor's whispered guesses. Were his lung issues asthma alone, or did he have tuberculosis like his father? The uncertainty left Algie feeling as though an invisible wall divided him from the rest of the world: those with time to waste and those without. If he wanted to achieve his dreams, he might have to work fast.

The motorboat stopped with a clang and a cough. Moments later, Frankie descended through the hatch.

"Hold tight." She yanked a lever on the wall.

CHAPTER

11

THE ROOM ROCKED. Algie grabbed a shelf for balance. Through the square opening in the floor, he caught the slop of shadowy water.

The room began to sink. Water rose to meet the open grate, lapping at its edges.

Algie pressed backward against the wall, fighting the urge to escape up the ladder. What was happening? They were going down!

"Don't worry," Lulu said, noticing his expression. "The water won't come in. Look behind you."

Water slurped and gurgled beyond the walls. Swallowing panic, Algie turned around.

The portholes opened on an underwater scene. Pilings stretched upward toward the surface. The pier made a black highway overhead. Strange shapes moved in the shadows beneath—fish relaxing in the cool water, hiding from the midmorning sun.

With a grinding of gears, the sinking laboratory juddered to a halt.

"But—what?" Algie stammered.

"It's a diving bell," Lulu said. "We're underwater!"

"Like being in a backward aquarium," said Frankie. "The fish are outside and the air stays in with us."

Algie stared at the opening in the floor. Not a drop of water had entered the room.

"Why doesn't the water pour through the hole?" he asked.

"The water pressure traps air inside," Frankie said. "If we went much deeper, it would flood the lab; but right now it fills the chamber underneath. This is one of the barges they used to build our deep-water pier. Papa customized it for us."

Algie peeked out a porthole. "That's the pier over there?"

"Where you landed yesterday," Frankie said. "Yell if you see a giant eyeball."

Excitement filled Algie as he realized his incredible opportunity. How many twelve-year-olds got to observe sea life from inside a real, functional diving bell? The researchers at the Chicago Academy of Natural History would jump at this chance! Fingers fumbling with eagerness, Algie dragged out his field notebook and began to scribble.

He could have taken notes for hours. But after fifteen minutes his nose was watering so badly that it dripped on the page. His chest constricted. He cleared his throat and coughed.

"Can you not do that?" Lulu asked as she hatched shadows across a half-finished sketch.

"Of course," Algie said. "Achoo!"

"Bless you."

"Thank you," Algie said. "ACHOO!" His forehead bounced off the porthole.

"Frankie . . ." Lulu bent over her paper. "I want to finish this drawing. Could you . . . ?"

Frankie sighed. "Come on, Algie. I'll show you the glass-bottom boat."

Algie followed Frankie up the ladder and back down onto the deck. She marched to the stern and turned an about-face.

"Able Seaman Algie," she said.

"Yes, Captain Frankie. I mean Francisca." Algie straightened his back.

"Can you swim?"

"No." Algie wondered if he were going to walk the plank.

"We'll fix that," Frankie said. "No landlubbers allowed aboard my ship."

The glass-bottom boat was a dinghy with a viewing pane in the bottom. Once Algie changed into his swimsuit, Frankie rowed to a spot close to the beach: shallow enough to stand, but beyond the roughest waves. She was a good teacher, and it was easier to get along when they had an immediate goal. The swimming lesson should have been fun. Surf-rippled sand, glinting water—best of all, he could dog-paddle by the end of it. But Algie's eyes burned, and his head throbbed. The burr in his chest got bigger. He could smell that harsh, caustic brine again.

"Are you all right?" Frankie asked, after a prolonged coughing fit by Algie.

"I swallowed some water." Algie gulped, his eyes streaming. If Frankie found out about his asthma, she would never let him into the FLEAS.

Frankie wasn't paying attention. She looked toward the beach. The undertow swirled her swim skirt around her knees.

"Is something burning?" she asked.

On the beach, gray haze rose diagonally on the wind. Two figures with wheelbarrows piled fuel on a smoldering heap.

Algie and Frankie splashed to shore.

"That's Gabe and Lenny. They're our security guards. I wonder what they're doing out here?" Frankie squinted as they neared the workers. Then her eyes widened.

The smoldering heap was composed of dead sea animals. Fish, eels, shorebirds . . . Algie turned away from a fire-blackened dolphin.

"What's going on?" Frankie demanded.

"Someone's got to clean up. There's nobody left to do it but us." The man she called Lenny removed his cowboy hat and wiped his forehead with a bandanna.

"Where did all these animals come from? Does the game-keeper know?" Frankie peered into a wheelbarrow of carcasses.

"It's the red tide," Gabe said. "And your pa fired the game-keeper two months ago, trying to save a paycheck."

"What's a red tide?" Algie whispered to Frankie.

"No one knows for sure." Gabe's biceps bulged as he flung a dead turtle onto the flames. "It usually comes in summer when the hotel is closed. Animals die, and sometimes the waves turn reddish. I don't know why it came this winter, but I wish it hadn't. Now folks are saying it's part of the curse."

"That's ridiculous," Frankie said. "Whoever heard of a seasonal curse?"

Algie sneezed again. His throat ached at the smoke.

"Thanks, Gabe—Lenny. Come on, Algie, let's get out of here." Frankie towed Algie back through the waves to the rowboat. She took the oars and began to row in short, choppy strokes.

"I'm sick of these northern tourists shooting off their mouths," she said. "They don't know anything about Florida."

Algie was about to reply, when a golfball-size eye flashed past the window in the bottom of the boat.

CHAPTER

12

ALGIE'S HEART BOUNDED—but the eye wasn't yellow. Whatever he had seen yesterday, this was not it.

The shape emerged from beneath the hull, longer than the rowboat. Frankie glanced over the side.

"That's Jasper," she said. "He's lived here the past couple seasons. Makes himself a nuisance because the tourists won't stop feeding him. It's a good thing he's easy to spot, because I'd hate to be in the water with him."

Algie couldn't agree more. His knees felt weak.

"What sort of shark is he?" he asked.

"A great hammerhead. See his wide flat face? And if he'll roll over and stop swimming on his side for a minute, you can see the characteristically long dorsal fin."

"Oh." Algie had trouble looking at anything besides Jasper's grinning mouth. And his size! To distract himself, he got out his field notebook.

"Great hammerhead shark: wide, flat head—"

WHUMP.

Frankie fell off her seat. Algie clutched the side. His umbrella hat toppled into his lap as Jasper's form blotted out the viewing port.

"Did he ram us?" Algie replaced his hat with shaky fingers.

"I think so." Regaining her oars, Frankie began to row. The *Diving Belle* was not far off.

WHUMP. This time, both Algie and Frankie fell against the same side of the boat. Water poured in as the edge slurped under. Frankie flung herself in the opposite direction, and the boat righted itself.

"Is this normal behavior?" Algie did not try to get back on his seat but stayed braced in the bottom of the boat.

"I think he wants food." Frankie's face whitened, her freckles standing out darker than usual.

Algie scanned the surface as they drew near the paddle barge. He could no longer disguise his wheezing. Each breath was a fight against the iron bands constricting his throat and chest.

As they drew alongside the *Diving Belle*, Frankie stood and caught the bottom rail. She pulled herself up and climbed over the railing onto the deck, then reached down to Algie.

"Come on!"

Algie was shaking, but not from fear. The bands around his chest had begun to close, as though someone were ratcheting them shut. He wrestled another breath and stood. The boat wobbled. He steadied himself against the side of the *Belle*.

"Hurry! He's headed this way again!" Frankie looked over Algie's head into the water. Summoning every ounce of energy, Algie reached up and grabbed the railing.

WHAM.

The empty boat bounced from beneath his feet. Algie dangled over the water, hanging on by the slippery rail. This was the moment in all the Professor Champion stories where the professor exerted his strength and wit and saved himself in the nick of time.

Algie tried. His muscles screamed, and so did his lungs. Frankie grabbed his wet wrists, too late. Algie's fingers peeled off the rail. His hands slid through Frankie's, and he plunged into water.

Weightless. Dizzy.

His head broke the surface. Through salt-blurred eyes, he saw Jasper shooting toward him.

A war cry sounded and Frankie hurtled through the air, wielding a boathook like a spear. The hook struck the shark on the snout. Frankie landed on Algie's head. He went under and surfaced again to see the boathook floating away.

Jasper wheeled, then doubled back. His fin raised a wake in the water. Algie shut his eyes. Something bumped hard against his leg. Algie kept his eyes shut, terrified he'd open them to find himself swimming in a cloud of his own blood.

A whooshing roar filled his ears. It seemed to be coming from above.

A heavy weight cascaded onto his head and scooped him into the air. His skull knocked against Frankie's. His teeth clacked together as his knees were crushed into his chest. The ocean spun sickeningly beneath them. They had been netted.

Algie and Frankie crashed onto a wooden deck in a puddle of rope and water. Still covered by the net, Algie wriggled out of his knapsack and yanked it open. With shaking hands, he undid the waterproof pouch and pulled out his Carbolic Asthma Ball. He put his mouth over the mesh-covered hole and squeezed. Powdered medicine filled his lungs. He squeezed again. Air in. Air out.

Slowly, the bands around his chest loosened.

His face pressed into the wet boards, Algie shut his eyes. He did not care where he was, or who had rescued him. All that mattered was glorious oxygen, filling his body with energy.

When his breathing grew easier, he opened his eyes. The left leg of his swimsuit was shredded as if by a cheese grater, but his skin was barely scratched. Frankie sat beside Algie, staring at him.

"Jasper," Algie wheezed. "He didn't—bite me."

"I thought he had." Frankie was pale beneath her suntan. Her pupils were huge.

Algie's stomach untwisted. Pulling the net off himself, he sat up, fumbled for his umbrella hat in the tangle of rope, and replaced it on his head.

They were on a swaying deck, ringed by polished railings. Wind hummed through the rigging, but—

Algie jumped to his feet. The ocean was twenty yards below, the *Diving Belle* a bobbing toy. The silken canopy of an immense balloon rippled overhead. That droning hum must be the noise of the power fan, and yes!—at the prow was that iconic figurehead featured in so many magazine illustrations! This was Professor Champion's famous airship, the *Flying Dancer*!

Algie whirled, blood pounding past his temples. At the airship's wheel stood a tall, powerful figure—a man in a safari helmet, with luxurious side-whiskers.

The would-be octopus killer of yesterday.

Frankie's voice dripped icicles. "Glad to see you back, Professor Champion."

The ground rocked beneath Algie's feet as a puff of wind shook the airship. Dazed, he put a hand to his umbrella hat.

"A young fan, I see." The professor glanced at Algie's hat. "Don't you know better than to wear that contraption in public? It's all right for the jungles of Darkest Peru, but you look a fool trotting about like that in civilization." He glanced again. "Why, you're the brat who stole my bait yesterday. If I'd known it was you, I'd have left you to the hammerhead." He spoke as though they were old acquaintances chatting over tea.

"What are you here to murder this year?" Frankie asked. "Bunnies? Puppies?"

In answer, the professor jerked the wheel sideways. Algie fell into Frankie as the airship tilted. Both stumbled onto a metal grating in the deck, which slid out from beneath them by some unseen mechanism. They fell six feet into darkness.

Gasping, Algie rubbed his bruised joints. He looked up at the checkered patch of sky where the grating ground back into place. He and Frankie were in a hold or storage area: dank, windowless, and filled with a musty sweetish smell. Slatted crates lined the walls. The mustiness seemed to be coming from them. It smelled like a dirty birdcage.

"Don't look." Frankie sighed as she pushed herself upright. But Algie had already gone over to the crates.

Glassy dead eyes stared out at him. Herons and egrets, their elegant necks twisted every which way, were piled in heaps like lifeless toys. Here and there, trickles of dried blood stained the brilliant plumage.

Algie stepped back. His mouth flooded as if he were going to throw up.

"That's not the worst of it." Frankie sat with her hands shading her eyes, avoiding the sight of the dead birds. "Usually plume hunters pick off nesting parents in rookeries and leave the babies to die. There's a lot of money in plume birds because they're so popular in ladies' hats. Lulu and I tried to rescue as many babies as we could last year, but it didn't turn out well."

"Does your father know?" Algie tried to shake off the image of an entire rookery of abandoned nests.

"Papa must have sold him a permit to hunt on our property. He did last season."

72

Professor Champion's voice floated down through the grating. "Even naturalists need to eat, you know. And pay for their airships."

Algie reached up, yanked the umbrella hat off his head, and crushed it between his fists.

CHAPTER

13

ALGIE STARED AT the ashes of his empty fireplace.

It had been noon when Professor Champion released them at the hotel. Algie had gone to his room, sat down without bothering to change his wet swimsuit, and had been sitting there ever since. Hours had passed. His skin felt crusted and sticky. His scratched leg throbbed.

Professor Champion, the hero Algie had admired and imitated. Now that was gone. Worse than gone—the Professor Champion he believed in had never existed. Algie felt as though a dear friend had died.

Everett's voice floated through his thoughts: "Mother thinks you should eat something."

Algie blinked. Everett stood beside the fire, holding a dinner tray and a glass of milk. He gazed over Algie's head with round, dreamy eyes.

"I've had the most wonderful day," he said.

"I'm glad someone did." Algie wished Everett would go away. He had no right to look so chipper after abandoning Algie that morning.

"You'd better get dressed if you want to come to the gala," Everett said. "Angel and the troupe are holding a special performance. All proceeds to benefit the prevention of cruelty to cab horses. I wouldn't miss it for the world."

"I didn't know you were so passionate about cab horses."

"I forgot to tell you!" Everett dropped the tray on the bedside table and bounced onto Algie's bed. "You'll never guess who's staying at the hotel—it's that naturalist fellow, Professor Champion! He's got the most glorious airship. I'd give anything for a ride on it—"

Algie clapped his hands over his ears. "Don't talk to me about Professor Champion!"

"Why not?" Cut short in his enthusiasm, Everett looked puzzled. "I thought you'd be thrilled."

"I would have been," Algie said. "Until I found out he's a fraud."

"You don't think he did all those things from the magazine stories? He looks like he could have."

"I didn't mean . . . " Algie paused. Fraud wasn't the right word. Professor Champion was every bit as experienced and resourceful as Algie had pictured him. Except he was nothing like Algie had pictured him.

"I guess he probably did," Algie said. "But it doesn't matter." His irritation at Everett lessened as he poured out the tale of the slaughtered plume birds. His brother would understand and sympathize.

Everett wrinkled his nose. "So you don't like him because he's a hunter?"

"What? No!" Algie thumped a pillow in frustration. "He's a naturalist—he should protect animals in danger! Francisca said whole populations of these birds have vanished from overhunting. If people aren't responsible, they could be wiped out."

"He has a permit," Everett said. "He isn't doing anything illegal."

Algie spluttered. "Just because it's *legal* doesn't mean it's right!"

"I know you're upset," said Everett, with an air of world wisdom, "but not everything is black and white."

"Starving baby birds so you can afford a fancy airship is!" Algie said. "Everett, he's cruel! You saw what he almost did to that octopus!"

"About that," Everett said. "I've been meaning to speak to you, Algie. What you did yesterday was out of line. I'm not saying Professor Champion was in the right, but it was his boat and his catch—"

"I don't care," Algie jutted his chin. "Stop acting like you're Father."

Everett raised his eyebrows. "You should care. Don't forget, *I* promised to keep you out of trouble. You're my responsibility.

And if I tell Mother you're too unreliable to go running around this hotel without her—"

The threat was too awful. Algie grabbed the glass of milk off the side table and emptied it over Everett's head.

Everett rose. Milk trickled down his collar as he collected his hat and stalked out the door joining the brothers' rooms.

After a minute, Algie got up and tried the handle. It was locked.

"Everett?" He knocked. No answer. Either Everett was ignoring him, or he was no longer in there.

Angry and guilty, Algie flumped on an armchair. He sank a foot into cushions and banged his head against a hanging lamp. Diamonds of light whirled around the room.

The whole day had been a disaster. Algie felt like a three-year-old whose sandcastle had been jumped on. Professor Champion was a bully, Everett hadn't apologized for abandoning him, and he'd blown his chance of getting into the FLEAS—Frankie would never tolerate a member who couldn't get through one swim lesson without an asthma attack. If it weren't for his asthma, he wouldn't have fallen into the water and nearly gotten them both killed. He shuddered as he remembered Jasper shooting toward him.

But . . . but . . . Jasper could have swallowed him whole if he had wanted. Algie should be dead, but he was alive. The room seemed to glow with new warmth.

Settling back into his squashy perch, Algie pulled over his dinner and opened his field notebook. He could make things right with Everett tomorrow.

"Arrival at the Hotel Paraíso," he said. "A Review." The pillows absorbed his voice.

"Day One: Yellow eye spotted in ocean. Stalked by unseen slithering creature in swamp. Angered wild boar. Lassoed by field biologists."

"Day Two—"

A splash in the bathroom jerked his eyes from the page.

Picking up volume five of Audubon's *Birds of America*, Algie crept toward the bathroom. He raised the book like a club and stepped into the room.

It was empty. The claw-footed bathtub stood regal and silent. The white walls gleamed behind their network of brass piping.

A small, sucker-lined arm emerged from the porcelain commode and waved. Two eyes peered out beneath the lid.

"You!" Algie picked up the octopus, dropped it into the sink, and gave it a rinse. The octopus wriggled, basking in the warm water. It was the same octopus from yesterday—the fishhook wound had not healed yet.

"It's nice to see you again," Algie said. "But what am I supposed to do with you?" The tram was out of commission, and a nighttime hike through the swamp to the beach did not sound like a good idea.

The octopus appeared to view this as Algie's problem. It hoisted itself out of the sink, shimmied down the piping, and slithered from the bathroom. It was surprisingly quick. Algie followed in time to see the last of its arms disappear beneath the door to the hall.

"Stop!" Algie ran after it. But when he opened the door, no octopus. Only an empty hallway, lined with blue wallpaper and candelabra.

A bubble of concern inflated within Algie's chest. He tried not to imagine the octopus wandering the hotel, parched for water, being skewered by some fashionable lady's high heel. Or what if Professor Champion discovered it?

A couple in evening dress passed down the hall. Algie held his breath. Would they spy the octopus and shriek for an exterminator? But the guests vanished around the corner without a fuss.

Algie was at a loss. Could the octopus have snuck beneath a different door already? Surely he would have seen it moving?

One of the unlit candelabra sprang to life and scampered away. With a shout, Algie pounded after it. What a finding! He had read that an octopus could mimic its surroundings, but hadn't realized it could be quite so good at it.

The octopus shambled through an open door. Algie zipped into the room and pounced.

"Got you!" He tucked it under his arm.

They were in a circular study lined with windows. A locked writing box, designed to hold pens and stationery, sat on a table scattered with papers.

Raised voices penetrated the wall, but Algie was too distracted by his recent observation to care. He went to the table. If he could scribble down a few notes on the way the octopus disguised itself . . . A pen stood in an inkwell. He set the octopus on the table and pulled over a sheet of blank paper.

"The octopus, which is able to survive for some time out of water, is a remarkable mimic. I myself observed—"

The octopus began using its suckers to explore the shiny gold lock on the writing box. It wasn't doing any harm, so Algie kept writing.

Until the locked box sprang open, displaying a compartment of letters. Algie grabbed for the box, but the octopus hung on to its new toy. Letters cascaded to the floor.

The study door banged open. An enormous figure filled the entrance.

CHAPTER

14

THE LADY IN the doorway wore a red-and-gold-sequined jacket, black boots, and plumed hat. She was tall and broad-shouldered. Algie had never seen such a solid-looking woman.

"What are you doing?" she demanded.

"I'm so sorry," Algie said. "I'm afraid my—pet—got into this box." He pried the octopus off the box.

"Your *pet*," the lady's nostrils flared, "got into my locked writing desk?"

"Yes, ma'am," Algie said. "It surprised me too. I think he picked the lock."

The woman's eyes roved around the room, searching out windows, cupboards, and fireplaces.

"You expect me to believe that?" She stooped to look under the sofa, and then checked behind a curtain. With a thrill of apprehension, Algie noticed a braided leather whip coiled at her belt.

"Not exactly," he said. "But that doesn't mean it didn't happen."

"Liar!" The woman skewered him with a glare. "Which one of them sent you?"

"I don't know what you mean." Holding the squirming octopus more tightly, Algie edged for the door. The woman grabbed at him. He dodged around the table.

"Those letters are my private correspondence!" the woman shouted. "What did you read?"

"Nothing," Algie said. "I—"

The woman threw the table aside. Algie ran for the door, but a strong hand caught the back of his swimsuit. He tried to squirm free but was hampered by the octopus.

"Madam Maximus," said a cool feminine voice. "I thought I heard the familiar sound of you shouting at someone."

Angel O'Dare stepped through the third-story window, wearing a red-and-gold-sequined bodysuit. Madam Maximus whirled, holding Algie by the scruff.

"Is this what you've sunk to? Sending children to spy on me?"

"Don't fool yourself." Angel's eyes narrowed. "I don't care what you do with your spare time."

"You'd give anything to see me out of business!"

"Wrong again," Angel said. "It's me who wants out of the business. Don't strangle that kid with his own swimsuit."

Madam Maximus released Algie, whom she'd been waving about for emphasis.

"Thank you," Algie gasped, massaging his throat.

Madam Maximus regained her composure. Her angry color faded. She folded her arms and turned on Angel. "I thought I told you to supervise warm-ups."

"Someone had to remind you that the performance starts in half an hour."

"I haven't lost the use of my memory, *thank* you," Madam Maximus snapped. But her hands shook as she smoothed her coat. She swayed and leaned against the table. Her face drained to a chalky color.

"Are you all right?" Algie ventured. Sometimes emotional stress brought on his asthma. Maybe this woman had a similar complaint—they were at a health resort, after all.

"Never been better." Madam Maximus's voice was not convincing. Pushing herself off the table, she picked up her writing box. Sweat beaded her forehead, despite the cool room.

"Now you've shouted yourself sick." Angel rolled her eyes, but her voice was not unkind. "Let me help you downstairs. I'll carry that box."

"NO!" Madam shouted, and even the octopus jumped. Gripping the box to her chest, she swept from the room.

"Catch me offering to help *her* again." Angel drummed her fingers on the table, her eyebrows creased. "You didn't happen to see what was in that box, did you, kid?"

"No," said Algie. "But I probably wouldn't tell you if I did."

"She's never had what you'd call a cherubic temper, but these days she's a lurking stack of dynamite." Angel chewed her lip, staring at the door where Madam had vanished. "I wish I knew what's got her tail in a knot."

"Don't you have a performance?" Algie asked.

"Right—thanks for reminding me." Angel shook her arms, stretched backward until she was almost bent in half, then sprang back to her original shape. She cartwheeled across the carpet and vaulted out the window.

Algie leaned against the sill as Angel bounced off an awning and caught a tree limb as though it were a trapeze. Swinging from branch to branch, she dropped to the ground.

But Algie could not stop seeing Madam Maximus's face as she'd turned away from Angel's aid. From his closer vantage point, Algie had seen what Angel could not—Madam's eyes wide with fear and misery.

"And I still don't know what to do with you," he said to the octopus.

Fortunately, he knew two people who might.

CHAPTER

15

AFTER CHANGING INTO more suitable attire, Algie made his way to the proprietor's landing and knocked at the girls' suite. The door opened to reveal Frankie.

"I brought you this." Algie held out the octopus.

"Thanks." Frankie took it. "Come in?"

Algie stepped into a room resembling a ship's cabin. Lulu sat cross-legged on a plain wooden table, while Hamlet the vulture presided from the mantlepiece. A lamp with a green shade cast light on several open books, a dictionary, pens, and paper.

"What are you studying?" Algie forgot his planned speech in curiosity. Knowing these two, it was probably interesting.

"We're working on our Spanish." Frankie unstuck the octopus as it tried to open her locket necklace. "If you have to know, we're not exactly fluent."

"Papa doesn't like to speak it with us," Lulu put in. "He says it's too sad."

"Why is it sad?" Algie asked. "It sounds like music."

"It makes him think of lost things," Lulu said. "Like Cuba, and Mama. Papa thinks it killed her to leave."

"Remind me why Cuba is lost?" Algie remembered something about a war.

Frankie assumed the air of a university professor. "Cuba is under Spanish rule and they're fighting for independence. We can't go back to Cuba because Papa's afraid we'll get shot. They shot José Martí not that long ago—the man who wrote these poems." She gestured at the book on the table.

Lulu caught Algie's look.

"Do you want us to translate?" she asked. "Frankie, read for him."

Frankie paged through the book.

"This one is about his wishes for a good death," she said. "It says 'I want to leave this world through the natural door: in a carriage of green leaves . . .' or does 'hojas' mean waves? No, that's 'olas . . . ' Hold on, I'll skip to my favorite bit." She cleared her throat and read in a firm voice: 'Do not put me in the dark to die like a traitor. I am good, and like the good, I will die with my face to the sun.'"

A short silence followed her words, broken by the crackling fire and Hamlet nibbling a steak bone.

"And did he?" Algie asked. "Die that way?"

"He died fighting for freedom," Frankie said. "Papa was furious. He said that as a patriotic poet, Martí could have done more good alive, and he should have stayed safe in the States. But I guess Martí thought there were more important things than living a safe life."

"Is that what the poem means?" Algie asked.

"I don't know," Frankie admitted.

Another silence followed. Algie remembered his errand. Out of habit, he reached for his umbrella hat, then remembered that he had crumpled it on board the airship.

"I've come to withdraw my application to the FLEAS." Why did he have to sound so stiff and formal? Why did his face feel like it was boiling?

"Don't be stupid," Frankie said. "We have equipment. We know how to get around without being stung, drowned, or eaten—most of the time, anyway. Why don't you want to join us?"

"I thought—" Algie cleared his throat. "I almost got you killed."

"You mean I almost got me killed. I don't jump on top of sharks for people I don't like."

Frankie liked him? This was news to Algie.

"I thought you didn't want me around," he said.

Frankie shrugged. "You're not scared to ask questions, and you don't back down from a challenge. I like that."

"But if you didn't like me, you wouldn't have jumped on Jasper." For some reason, Algie did not find this reassuring.

"Why should I?" Frankie seemed genuinely puzzled.

"Algie, Frankie told me you got sick all of a sudden," Lulu said. "What happened?"

Algie explained. About his asthma. How he had to take medicine every day, carry medicine everywhere. How important it was that he become a real naturalist and contribute to the world before he ran out of time. How Florida was supposed to help him get better, but his asthma attack this morning had been the worst he'd had in years.

Lulu wrinkled her forehead. "I had a sore throat and itchy eyes myself, sitting in that diving bell. Do you think the red tide could be affecting us somehow? Only it's worse for you, because of your lungs?"

"You weren't in the water," Frankie objected. "Algie and I were, but I felt fine."

"She could be right, though," Algie said. "I've heard they're working on aerosolized inhalation therapies—liquid medicine they atomize so you can breathe it. Do you think sea spray could produce something like that? A breathable version of whatever toxin is making the sea animals sick?"

"It's an interesting hypothesis," Frankie said. "But we need to focus on stopping the curse. If we can't do that, we won't be here to study the red tide."

Lulu pouted. "You don't like the idea because you didn't come up with it."

"A good naturalist doesn't let herself get distracted. And speaking of distractions, we were supposed to be at the gala fifteen minutes ago."

CHAPTER

16

"'OCTOPUS' IN SPANISH is 'pulpo,'" Lulu said, settling the octopus into the girls' saltwater aquarium. "Let's call him Pulpy for short. We'll bring him to the beach tomorrow."

With Pulpy safe in his temporary home, they reached the lawn before the circus troupe finished their parade around the grounds. Slashes of sunset through the trees lent an eerie smolder to the scene, and a smoky haze of fireworks hung on the air. Ribbon twirlers pirouetted beneath arcs of juggled swords, lit by the whirling glow of fire dancers.

At the head of the procession sat Madam Maximus on a thronelike chair held aloft by the strongman. Her hands were not shaking anymore. Her eyes roved the crowd.

Last of all came Angel O'Dare, neither twirling, tumbling, nor juggling. Her flamelike mask and bodysuit matched those of the other acrobats, complete with the double "M" symbol Algie had seen on the triple-masted ship at the ocean dock. He clapped along with the other guests as the troupe passed through the outdoor entrance to the swim hall. As the crowd followed the acrobats up the marble steps, Algie paused for a last look across the grounds.

The music and cheering seemed to fade.

On the far side of the lawn, a line of iridescent lights swirled through the water at the edge of the lake.

Algie grabbed Frankie's elbow.

"What?" Distracted, Frankie slipped and half-fell against the steps, catching herself with her hands. "Ouch!"

Algie looked back. The fairy lights had vanished.

"What?" Frankie repeated, brushing her hands on her skirt.

Algie bit his lip. Had Frankie missed the lights, or was his medicine making him see things again?

"I'll tell you later," he said. He followed Frankie up the stairs.

Inside, dim lights directed spectators to their seats. Otherwise, the swim hall was dark.

"Forget seats," Frankie whispered. She steered them to the marble diving platform where the orchestra had played last night. Algie stretched his legs and breathed the cool scent of wet stone and water. His apprehension vanished in a thrill of anticipation.

Harp music trickled from the gallery. The gathered crowd hushed. A spotlight illuminated Angel O'Dare, floating in a gondola in the center of the pool. Dark water shimmered around her.

A hoop dropped from the darkness, sliding down the beam of light until it stopped above Angel's head. She pressed into a handstand and arched her back over the hoop. The spotlight followed as she whirled into the air.

For the next hour, Algie forgot curses and illnesses, disappointing professors and overbearing brothers. Spotlights illuminated a network of tightropes strung high above the pool. Acrobats flipped from trapezes and twirled off aerial silks, glittering as they performed one astounding feat after another. Algie caught his breath along with the crowd as a chain of trapeze artists swung through the air. One muscular acrobat tossed Angel higher than seemed possible. She caught a pair of flying rings and whirled in a circle, then flipped down to pull him up with her. Madam Maximus conducted the scene from aloft, snapping her ringmistress's whip as she revolved inside a great golden hoop.

By the end of the show, Algie was wrung out with breathlessness and awe. He wondered what it must be like to have a body that worked so perfectly, obeying his every thought. Then he felt remorseful. His own body did its best. It was not its fault it happened to have asthma.

Too soon it was time for the finale. A pyramid of acrobats rose into the air, bigger individuals balancing on tightropes as the smaller performers scrambled onto their shoulders. They enveloped Madam Maximus's hoop, and the ringmistress disappeared beneath a framework of red-and-gold bodies. Unseen drums beat a restless tattoo, quickening Algie's pulse.

Cymbals clashed, and Madam Maximus vaulted into the air. The pyramid of acrobats unfolded as Madam twirled and spun. She spiraled back down through the web of equipment and sliced into the pool with barely a splash.

The crowd erupted in applause. Algie stood alongside Frankie and Lulu as acrobats slid down their silks and landed next to the pool to take their bows. Slowly, the lights rose.

The applause faltered and turned to gasps of horror.

Madam Maximus clawed her way out of the pool, wiping frantically at a dark liquid on her skin and clothes. She was glittering no longer.

"My eyes," she gasped. "I can't see!"

The pool was filled not with water, but with ink.

CHAPTER

17

HOURS LATER, ALGIE couldn't sleep. He flopped onto one side, then the other. Madam Maximus had recovered her vision after an eye bath, but the image of the black pool was stamped on Algie's mind. Horrified guests, vowing to leave in the morning . . . Algie couldn't blame them. That inky expanse had seemed to hold a threat. Something was going on, something big and out of control. Or was it as simple as corroded pipes discoloring the water? Most importantly—would his mother want to leave?

Thump.

Algie's mind thudded into alert. He wasn't alone in the room.

Calm down, Algie told himself. He was on edge like everyone else, ready to be frightened. Probably the noise had been made by a staff member dropping a suitcase in the hall.

But Algie could not shake the feeling of a shadowy presence. In the dim moonlight, the furniture loomed like ghosts.

Something slithered over his ankles.

Algie screamed, yanking his feet to his chin. The hotel really was haunted! There was a monster in his room!

Frankie and Lulu burst through the doorway. Lulu pounced on the foot of the bed while Frankie dive-tackled Algie.

"Shhh!" She muffled him with a pillow.

"He got out of the tank." Lulu held up Pulpy the octopus. "I don't know how, because we stacked a whole set of encyclopedias on the lid. We thought he might come visit you."

"He's smart," Frankie said. "He must remember you rescued him."

"That's nice," Algie gasped. His heart was galloping through his ears.

"What time is it, anyway?" Frankie slid off the bed and went to the window. "And what is *that*?"

Algie jumped up. The familiar line of ghost lights rippled across the lawn, floating over the grass toward the greenhouse.

"I saw those earlier this evening!" he whispered. "Right before the performance!"

Nightgowns and pajamas flapped around their ankles as the three of them raced downstairs. A breeze rocked shadows across the lawn, clattering the palm fronds. When they reached the greenhouse, the gates stood ajar.

"Off limits to guests except by special permission," read a placard dangling from the wrought-iron spirals.

"Do I have permission?" Algie asked Lulu.

"As long as you stick with Frankie and me." Lulu handed him Pulpy as she slid a machete knife from beneath her bathrobe.

"You keep knives in your pajamas?"

"When I run around after midnight during curses, I do."

"You can't use a machete on a ghost," Algie objected.

Lulu hefted the blade. "You can try."

The air was hot, stagnant, and humid. Stepping inside the greenhouse was like ducking under a thick blanket. Broken glass glimmered on a path choked with overgrown plants.

"Stay close behind me." Frankie uncoiled her lasso from her bathrobe belt. "And don't leave the path unless I do."

Lulu motioned Algie ahead of her as Frankie ducked beneath a palm frond. Her machete blade flashed in the moonlight.

"What do you think is in here?" Algie whispered, hanging back to speak to Lulu. She poked him with the hilt of her knife to hurry him along.

"I don't know what else is here, but I think alligators will have moved into the decorative fountain—we call it the Fountain of Youth—by now. And I'm almost certain some macaque monkeys that escaped from the old menagerie come back here to visit, so keep an eye on the treetops."

Algie tried to move quietly as he followed Frankie, ducking and twisting between roots and branches.

"What's that?" he whispered.

A tangled mass of flowers and vines spiraled into the air toward a dim upper gallery.

"It's a staircase," said Frankie. "You can't tell because of the climbing plants."

"What happened to this place?"

"The same thing that happened to the topiary bushes," Lulu said. "Papa couldn't afford enough gardeners, so the jungle took over."

Algie halted to avoid running into Frankie, who had frozen in the shadow of a palmetto.

"What?" he whispered.

"Shh!"

Algie held his breath, hugging Pulpy to his chest. A gentle sloshing noise lapped against his ears. It sounded like ripples against a bank. Something alive, moving through water.

A suckered arm gripped his wrist, and he swallowed a yelp. Pulpy was prying his fingers loose. Algie grabbed at him, but the octopus slithered from his grasp and flopped to the ground.

"Stop," Algie whispered. "It might be alligators—Pulpy!" as Pulpy scrambled off the path and dove into the undergrowth.

Algie plunged after him. He knew it would make noise, but nothing prepared him for the shaking, snapping, and clattering that rose as he fought his way through the brush.

The garden lights switched on. Where before there had been darkness and dancing shadows, strands of lightbulbs and globe-shaped lanterns blazed into existence. Thousands of butterflies took to their wings, filling the air with confusion. The effect was blinding, and at first Algie did not realize he had almost stumbled into a large, decorative pool. A shout rose at the far side of the conservatory.

Frankie and Lulu burst from the bushes.

"Who yelled?" Frankie demanded. "Did you turn on the lights?" Water slopped over the sides of the Fountain of Youth, as if a swimmer had recently exited. A fierce crackling came from the bushes on the far side of the fountain. It was moving toward them.

Frankie shook out her lasso. Lulu dropped to a crouch, her machete raised. Algie clasped his hands and tried not to let his heart pound him off his feet.

Angel O'Dare stepped from the thicket. Her eyes shone with triumphant light.

"I saw it," she said.

CHAPTER

18

EXCITED VOICES HUMMED throughout the breakfast room.

"Haunted, beyond doubt!"

"I didn't hear 'haunted,' I heard 'cursed.'"

"Miss O'Dare saw it with her own eyes. A sea serpent the length of a football field, slithering from the fountain."

"She told me it was a giant ape with a dragon's tail. Almost squeezed the life out of her before she clocked it on the snout with her parasol."

"We're leaving on the ten o'clock steamer. The Ponce de Leon Hotel in St. Augustine is more fashionable, and I've never heard of cursed kelpies crawling around it."

Algie sat at a table with Mrs. Emsworth, Everett, and Lord Plumworthy. He turned to Everett, hoping his brother had forgotten their fight over Professor Champion the night before.

"What do you think of Angel's story?" he asked.

Everett chewed a bite of toast before answering.

"I think," he said, "that Miss O'Dare saw whatever she said she saw. If it's a creature of some kind, Professor Champion will handle it."

"Yes, but what *did* she say?" Algie asked. "I've heard twelve different descriptions in the last five minutes."

"Are you calling her a liar?" Everett threw down his napkin. Mrs. Emsworth looked up.

"Everything all right, darlings?" she asked.

"Yes, Mother." Everett folded the napkin and placed it by his plate. "That reminds me—Miss O'Dare introduced me to Professor Champion last night. He offered to show me around his airship. I said I wouldn't mind helping out if he needed anything."

"What?" Algie gasped. Despite their different opinions, he had never dreamed that Everett would stoop to hobnob with the professor. "Everett, you can't! That would make you in league with him!"

Everett knocked his fork off the table with an elbow, the signal for a private word with Algie. Together, they ducked to retrieve it.

"Listen up," Everett whispered under cover of the table-cloth. "I won't go around knocking baby birds on the head, but I

100

will do anything else, and I mean *anything*, to get on board that airship. This is the chance of a lifetime! Who knows? He might even teach me to fly it!"

"Fine!" Algie hissed. "Be a traitor and a—an accomplice! Even if you don't care about the professor's marauding, I thought you cared about me. I guess I was wrong."

Everett went blotchy with anger. Algie stuck out his tongue. Both boys jerked upright, bumping their heads on the table.

"If you ask me," said Lord Plumworthy as he took another roll, "all this monster business is nonsense."

"You're saying Angel imagined it?" Everett rubbed his head, grimacing.

"Of course not. But if there is a monster, or a curse, there's no reason why it should get in the way of fishing. Has anyone seen my wife?"

"She's upstairs, getting ready," Mrs. Emsworth said. "Mr. Davenport is arranging glass-bottom boat monster tours at special last-minute prices."

Angel O'Dare entered the solarium.

"There she is!" Everett bounced from his seat and scuttled across the room. Snatches of one-sided conversation drifted over the sardines and marmalade.

"A delight to watch you perform last night—yes, the professor and I—if I might have the pleasure—join me this afternoon in a round of golf?"

Everett's rival, Mr. Parker James, wavered as if meaning to head toward the twosome, but thought better of it. Algie, however, placed his napkin near his plate, excused himself, and marched over to them.

"Did you really describe all those monsters people are talking about?" he asked Angel.

"Get lost," said Everett. Algie waited for Angel's answer.

Angel yawned, fanning her mouth. "Of course not. Like I told you last night, I saw a black thing like an enormous snake's tail wiggling out of a broken pane in the greenhouse. It was about twenty feet long."

Algie kept his eyes on her. Angel looked out the French windows, avoiding his gaze. Algie wasn't sure he believed she hadn't started those stories. She didn't seem the type to let her imagination run away with her—if Angel had spread those rumors, she'd done it deliberately. Could she have lied about the whole thing? Did she want the hotel to close?

"ANGEL!"

Madam Maximus strode through the tables, scattering breakfasters. Clearly her adventure the night before had done nothing to sweeten her temper. Angel listened to the tirade with half-lidded eyes, her jaw sullen.

"I'll have the law on you for breach of contract if I catch you skipping practice again. No, I would NOT like a cup of coffee!" Madam swept Angel away.

"All hands on deck!" Lulu dashed up to Algie, dragging Frankie by the elbow. "We've got to start early, before Professor Champion!"

"Hey!" Everett shouted after them. "I know you kids were wandering around the greenhouse last night. Stay out of places you don't belong—I mean it!"

"Like we don't belong in our own greenhouse," Frankie snorted, as they collected their gear. "You snowbirds wouldn't know a crocodile from an alligator if it bit you on the ankle, so you think everyone else is in the same boat."

"Leave me out of this." Algie raised his voice louder than he meant to. "A crocodile has a slimmer snout and you can see its teeth more easily."

"Touchy this morning, are we?" Frankie hoisted her pack higher on her back.

Grass, gravel, and the weathered gray sides of the boathouse sparkled beneath a sheen of dewdrops as they hurried down the lawn toward the headspring. Algie's legs felt rubbery. His head was swimming from his morning medicine. The picnic basket he and Lulu carried between them banged against his legs and threatened to drag his arm off.

If Frankie or Lulu were tired, they did not show it. Both wore heavy canvas rucksacks, and Frankie's eyes fairly sizzled with fanaticism.

"Aren't you worried?" Algie puffed. "If guests are leaving—"

"If we find the monster before the hotel closes, they'll come back," Frankie said. "We'll survey the backwaters for anything unusual. Tonight we stake out the greenhouse, and maybe that spring where you saw the boar, Algie. We could try and lure the monster with bait, but some of these big snakes don't eat for months between meals—"

"Is that what we think it is?" Algie set down the picnic basket to rub his arm. "A giant snake?"

"There've been rumors about massive snakes in this swamp for ages," said Lulu. "People say the Señora imported South American anacondas to guard her moat, and when she died they escaped and kept growing."

"Who's the Señora?"

"An inventress who lived here at the end of the eighteenth century. Part of the hotel is built around her villa."

Algie nodded, and frowned as his mind went back to anacondas.

"What about the ink in the pool?" he asked. "A snake couldn't do that. And those lights, and the dead creatures on the beach. It must all be connected. But how?"

"I'll tell you how." Frankie leaned forward. "Professor Champion!" She crossed her arms and stepped back, waiting for the effect of her thunderbolt.

But Algie could not oblige her with awestruck wonderment.

"What do you mean?" he said.

"Don't you see?" Frankie began talking fast, waving her hands. "It's all a dastardly plot of Professor Champion's! He's brought back this snake, or whatever it is, from one of his travels and set it loose on our grounds. He spreads the rumor of a monster, gets people worked up about a curse, recaptures it himself, and, hey, presto—another best-selling magazine article! But," she said, growing calmer, "we're going to stymie him, because *we're* going to catch it first and take all the credit. They'll be writing magazine articles about *us*!"

Algie thought this over.

"What's your evidence?" he asked.

"I don't need any! The man's a villain; you've seen what he's capable of!"

"Sure," Algie said, "but you still need evidence before you accuse him of letting a monster loose at a resort."

Frankie's nostrils flared.

"So," she said. "You're defending him?"

"No!" Algie yelped. "I would never do that! I'm saying—"

Off to the side, Lulu gave her head a shake. *Don't bother*, her expression warned.

Algie bit his lip. He wanted to argue with Frankie, who was clearly letting her dislike of the professor cloud her judgment. But if he got on her bad side, she might ban him from their expeditions. Yesterday she had said nice things about him. If he spoke up, he would lose that good opinion.

"You were saying?" Frankie stuck out her jaw.

Algie shook his head. "Nothing."

"Wait until you see the swamp skimmer, Algie," Lulu broke in. "It's modeled after one of the Señora's prototypes. Papa had it built back when we staffed our own inventors. We have a lot of her sketches and notebooks in the library. She was a distant relation of Papa's."

From the open boathouse came the sputter of an engine. A swear word dropped from Frankie's lips, and she broke into a run. Algie and Lulu followed, hampered by the heavy picnic basket.

An egg-shaped craft bobbed in a docking bay. It looked like the illustration of the *Nautilus* in Algie's copy of *Twenty Thousand Leagues*, only smaller and floating on top of the water. Professor Champion stood at the helm.

"Hey!" Frankie banged on the hull. "This isn't your boat! We're using her today."

"It's your father's boat, and I am paying him to rent it, as I have already paid him to hunt on these grounds." Though muffled, Professor Champion's voice boomed through the glass. "I'm going to collect this beast of Miss O'Dare's. And if I catch one of you brats within a five-mile radius, I'll pop you with my tranquilizer gun and strap you to the roof for a six-hour nap."

He cranked the throttle. The engine roared. Jets of water spurted from beneath the egg-craft as it peeled out of the boathouse, showering the children with water.

"We have to get to that monster before he does." Frankie shook oily drops from her hair.

Algie nodded. Regardless of Frankie's theory about the professor, she was right on one thing: if they introduced this mystery creature to the world, there would be magazine articles written about them. It was their chance to catch the eye of the scientific community. If the tail Angel had seen was

106

over twenty feet long, who knew how large the whole animal might be?

"We'll have to take the waterbugs." Frankie pointed to a trio of what looked like floating bicycles with flat bottoms instead of wheels. Large fan-motors were mounted to the backs.

"It's a steep learning curve," Lulu said to Algie. "But we'll practice in the headspring where there's less chance of gators."

CHAPTER

19

THEY WERE ABOUT to speed straight into solid land. As they whizzed toward the green bank, Algie shut his eyes.

The crash never came. Algie opened his eyes and ducked in time to dodge a low-flying spoonbill. The bank was a bed of aquatic plants, only their tops rising above the surface. Reeds squeaked and flattened beneath his hydrofoil.

The watercraft wobbled, and he steadied the handlebars. He could see why these contraptions were called "waterbugs." Without keels or rudders, they could skim through the shallowest backwater but overbalanced at the slightest miscalculation. The sisters had made him practice in deep water for over an hour before they let him into the bayous. At least the fresh water didn't seem to affect his lungs the way the ocean had.

Frankie cut her engine and skidded sideways to stop beside a mudbank. Algie overshot and had to double back.

"That's strange." Lulu wrinkled her nose.

To Algie, it looked like the thousand other mudbanks they had passed that morning.

"Did a giant snake slither ashore here?" he asked.

"It wasn't a snake," Frankie said. "I don't know *what* it was."

Algie started to dismount, but the girls' simultaneous "STOP!" halted him.

"Don't get into the water," said Lulu, regaining her calm. "We're right in the heart of Hell's Pocket, and it has more alligators than the rest of the property put together."

"Really?" Algie asked.

"Not literally," Frankie said. "But there are a lot. Stay on your bug."

A school of fish flashed through a patch of sunlight. Algie shaded his eyes with his hand. "Aren't those the same sort of fish we saw in the diving bell yesterday?"

"Those are euryhaline fish," Frankie said. "A euryhaline organism can live in both saltwater and fresh water. If the ocean water is bad right now, they might be swimming upriver to get away from it."

"Can octopi live in salt and fresh water too?" This question had been bothering Algie all day. They hadn't been able to find Pulpy last night, and it was a long way to the ocean.

"Octopuses are strictly marine animals." Frankie restarted her fan-engine.

"Don't worry," Lulu called over the noise. "Any octopus smart enough to pick a lock is a pretty remarkable animal. You lost him in the swamp once before. I'm sure he'll be fine."

They sped through the swamp again. Left turn—dodge an island—right turn. The bayous branched and rebranched until Algie wondered how the girls could keep track. Leaf shadows whirled in dizzy flickers across the surface.

Whap!

A sticky net plastered itself over Algie's face. The occupant, a huge banana spider, thunked into his forehead.

"*Ack!*" Algie swatted at the web gumming his eyes and hair. His fingers found the spider, and he threw it as far as he could. His waterbug careered across the bayou, straight toward a knobbly cypress knee.

Algie clawed the web out of his eyes and wrenched the handlebars around. His waterbug skidded almost on its side but missed the root. Regaining his balance, Algie cut the throttle, but inertia carried him forward.

Then Algie saw the turtle, scrambling along an overhanging branch. That couldn't be right—turtles didn't climb trees. Or maybe they did at the Hotel Paraíso. Oddity seemed the norm here.

As Algie whooshed beneath, the turtle toppled from its perch.

Clonk.

Algie fell backward. The water's impact knocked him breathless. The riderless waterbug smashed into a tree, and the fan-motor snapped from its mount. The fuselage somersaulted through the air and sank.

Shaking, Algie splashed to the nearest land. His back and shoulders stung. Who knew water could feel so solid? A turtle-size lump throbbed on his forehead. The turtle in question was paddling off, presumably in search of a more peaceful tree. No sign of Frankie or Lulu. Only the whine of two waterbugs fading in the distance.

Algie hoped he hadn't taken a wrong turn during his grapple with the banana spider. If not, it was a simple matter of waiting until the girls noticed his absence and doubled back. However, he had noticed that neither Frankie nor Lulu were in the habit of looking behind them.

"Hello?" he called.

The swamp seemed to swallow his words.

He stood on a narrow island hissing with plume grass. The river lay waist-deep on either side, tea-color lightening to caramel where sunlight sifted through the branches. Fish hovered close to the silty bottom, their bodies blending with waterweed.

Movement caught Algie's eye. A five-foot alligator glided through the water, moving with almost imperceptible sweeps of its tail. At the last minute it changed its mind and veered away from his island.

Sweat sprang up on Algie's palms. He gripped the handle of the machete Frankie had given him at the start of the expedition.

Maybe he should cross the bayou and climb one of those trees. Yes—the more he thought about it, the more sensible it seemed. Of course it meant getting into the water and stumbling around on the bank. A hundred alligators might be hiding in those roots. But it was better than standing out in the open.

The reeds on Algie's island whispered. He looked behind.

An enormous alligator's head slid through the grass two feet away.

The chitter of a nearby squirrel made a mockery of Algie's predicament. The alligator must have been on the island all along. Had it been stalking him this whole time?

The gator tipped its snout and hissed. *Get off my island*, it seemed to be saying.

Algie had two options. Cross the river and hope it wouldn't follow, or attack with his machete. The alligator was so huge it looked fake, its skin thick and black as rubber. Only the yellow eyes seemed alive.

But Algie was not fooled. He knew it could move much faster than he could, and his machete would be nothing against that armored hide. Could he leap onto its back and hold its mouth shut? No—much as he hated to admit it, he didn't have the skill for such a move. It would be madness to antagonize this prehistoric monster. He was stuck with the most practical and terrifying option—stay calm and back off.

Eyes on the alligator, Algie stepped back.

But the gator had lost patience. Hoisting its body off the ground, it charged. Algie whirled and flung himself into the water. His foot sank into a hole, and his knee overextended. He fell forward onto his stomach.

Clawed legs shoved Algie underwater as the alligator's jaws slammed shut on his backpack. Algie tried to wriggle free, but his arms caught in the straps.

The alligator rolled. There was no up or down: only blinding, choking water in his eyes and lungs. Algie's ribs inhaled and more swamp water flooded his lungs, sending him into spasms of panic. His mind spun too—was he dying? His mother would never know what had become of him—

Suddenly the alligator was wrenched from his back. Algie didn't have time to wonder before the spots behind his eyes gathered into a snowstorm and whirled him into unconsciousness.

CHAPTER

20

ALGIE WOKE WITH a crawfish clamped on to his tongue.

"Ouch!" He hurled it away. The crustacean sailed a few feet and plopped into the water.

Slowly, Algie's eyes and mind adjusted to his surroundings.

A pillar of light from a hole in the cave's ceiling illuminated an underground pool so clear, Algie could see the nostrils on an alligator's skull twenty feet below. He lay on a shelf of rock dotted with mossy, football-size stones. Across the cave-pool rose a tottering structure of rocks, branches, and other objects piled to make a kind of mound or grotto. There were pieces of wooden railing, a birdbath, a rowboat, and a broken garden statue of a mother and child.

Algie's skin tingled, and his temples began to thump. He had not magically appeared in this cave, nor had that grotto built itself.

It wasn't a grotto, he realized. It was a nest.

Algie got to his feet and backed toward the wall of the cave, slipping on the shallow sheet of water and fuzzy algae. All his being stayed focused on that dark structure in the center of the pool. His hands and back met the wall. It felt strangely rubbery.

Something tapped his shoulder. Another crawfish was inserted gently but insistently into his mouth.

Algie turned.

Two yellow eyes glared from the shadows as an odd pattern of seams in the wall peeled from the rock and reached outward. It was a massive octopus, the exact color of the limestone.

A scream ripped through Algie's mind as every nerve fought to shriek, dive, and splash away from the monster. But in the center of the scream was a quiet place that knew escape was impossible. Using every ounce of his willpower, Algie planted his feet and gazed into the octopus's eyes. Its black-barred pupils stared back into his soul.

A fifty-foot-long arm of pure muscle extended over Algie's head. Algie didn't move as the octopus paused, snatched, and lifted a yellow-and-brown fish from the water. Holding the thrashing fish delicately between suckers, the octopus tucked it beneath its mantle. When the fish appeared again, it hung limp and still.

The octopus proffered the fish to Algie.

"Thank you," Algie said. "I've already eaten." He set the fish down by his feet.

One by one, the round stones dotting the ledge somersaulted, changed color, and extended stubby arms. Seven little octopi swarmed the fish, while the eighth ascended Algie's leg.

"Pulpy!" Algie hugged him.

Two small octopi became tangled and rolled over, silently wrestling. The big octopus turned red and plucked the grapplers apart. Fascinated, Algie squatted to watch. The octopi moved like dancers, always with a piece coiling or uncurling even while the rest of their body was still. They're babies, Algie realized.

"Pulpy," he said. "You're a baby giant octopus."

The mother octopus flushed pink, watching him admire her brood. Bioluminescent spots gleamed along her sides in the shadows — like the "ghost lights" Algie had seen the night before.

Leaves crunched above, and a voice sifted down through the hole in the ceiling.

"What are we going to do, Lulu?" Could that be Frankie? She sounded close to tears.

"Algie is smart. I don't believe a gator got him. He probably found a safe place to wait, and we missed it."

"We shouldn't have brought a greenhorn city kid on such an important expedition. I told you we should have said we were busy today."

"We couldn't leave him out. We agreed to give him a chance!"

"Well, that's not looking like such a good decision, is it?" Frankie's voice was sharp. "He can barely balance on his own two feet, much less—"

After the morning he'd had, this was too much. Algie pressed the heels of his hands against his eyes, willing the tears to stay inside. No matter how hard he worked, it would never be enough. Frankie's words stung like a slap. But she hadn't said anything untrue. He *was* clumsy and new to the swamp.

Algie struggled for perspective. Maybe he could not twirl a lasso, climb a rope, or wield a machete as well as the Floridian sisters—all right, he could not twirl, climb, or wield them at all. But his mother had always told him a person's worth didn't lie in their skills. Not even in their success, however worthy the career. Was his inner measure up to snuff, even if his biceps were not?

With a start, he realized the voices were fading. Tagging along with two people who didn't want him was better than starving to death in a cave.

Algie inflated his lungs.

"Hi!" he bellowed. The baby octopi froze, changing color to match the rock ledge.

"Hello?" someone called.

"I'm down here," Algie yelled.

"It's Algie!" Lulu shrieked, as Frankie shouted "Down where?"

It took a few minutes of back-and-forth before they could locate his position. After the first few shouts, the octopi unfroze and went about their business. The little ones resumed chasing each other up and down the walls, and the mother slipped into the water to tidy her nest.

The outline of a head appeared in the cave opening.

"Algie?"

Frankie's eyes squinched and her hair hung around her face. Algie realized she could not see far into the dim cave, positioned as she was and surrounded by bright sunshine. And then came the idea—an idea that burned and squeezed his chest, speeding up his heartbeat.

He would not tell the sisters of his discovery. He could make up a story to keep them from entering the cave—tell them it was teeming with vampire bats or fragile nesting birds or something. They would lower a rope to haul him out. Later he could come back alone, learn the secrets of the octopi, and burst onto the scientific world with dazzling brilliance.

But . . . the girls had been kind to him, even if he was useless. Frankie had jumped on a shark for him.

No! This was his discovery. They had no right to steal his glory. Frankie was too arrogant, she deserved to be knocked down a peg. Neither of them was sick, they had time—

"Algie?" Frankie's voice was uncertain.

Algie squashed his ego and sat on it.

"Come down," he said. "There's something you'll want to see."

CHAPTER

21

POOF.

Frankie emerged from behind her box camera.

"The distinguished naturalist, Professor Algernon Emsworth, poses with his stupendous find," she said. "I'll develop these photos tonight."

Lulu sat on the wet ledge, sketching as best she could with three baby octopi in her lap. She waved away the garfish Mother Octopus kept pressing on her guests.

"Did we decide on a scientific name?" she asked.

"*Octopus giganteus*," Algie said. "*Octopus* for the genus, and *giganteus* for 'giant.'"

Frankie leaned sideways. "Have you two noticed the bottom of this pool?"

Algie and Lulu looked over the edge.

Bones. Not a few, but bones everywhere, littering the bottom of the spring. Alligator skulls were easy to pick out, but many others Algie had trouble recognizing. Waterweed blanketed the sunken graveyard, shimmering with tiny bubbles.

Frankie studied the bones with detached concentration.

"I don't think the octopuses ate all these," she said. "Most of the skeletons look like they've been here for ages."

"How did they get here?" Algie asked.

"Fell in, is my guess. Over hundreds of years."

"Couldn't the octopi have been eating them for hundreds of years?"

"I don't think they've been here that long," Lulu said. "All these Mysterious Happenings—I think it must have been the octopuses. The ink in the swimming pool, the Thing that grabbed Madam Maximus . . . even those boards over there look like part of the tramway. She must have been collecting for her nest."

Revelation flashed in Algie's mind. "That slithering I heard by the spring the first day—it was her! And those things I thought were rocks were the camouflaged babies. She must have paralyzed the boar with her toxic nip and tucked him in the tree."

"I don't blame her," Frankie said. "Those boars can get aggressive."

"Do you think the octopi might be running from the red tide?" Algie asked. "Like the fish we saw earlier?"

"That's good thinking." Frankie looked envious that she hadn't come up with the hypothesis. "I've never heard of a euryhaline octopus, but I've never heard of one that cares for its babies either. I bet that's why she pulled the alligator off you, Algie. It's usually social animals that go out of their way to help humans—ones that live in groups, like dogs and dolphins."

"Pulpy was in the ocean when I found him," Algie said. "And he was sick—all white and lethargic. I thought it was from being hooked by Professor Champion, but maybe it was the red tide. I wonder if he tried to go home. He doesn't seem to like to stay put."

"Yes, you have your eight arms full, don't you?" Frankie stroked the mother octopus's rubbery skin. The octopus stroked Frankie's face. "What should we call her?"

"Helen," Algie said. "After Helen of Troy, because she's so beautiful."

"Don't be sappy. How about Hippolyta?"

"Octavia." Lulu shut her sketchbook.

"Octavia," Algie said. "I like that. What about the rest of the octopi?"

"You can stop calling them 'octopi,' for starters," Frankie said. "That's a word mashed together from Greek and Latin that makes no sense."

"I'm using it in English, not Greek or Latin," said Algie, annoyed. "And it's what my natural history books use."

"Your natural history books are wrong."

"What do you mean, 'wrong?' Do you think English always makes sense?"

"If you're using it in English," Frankie said, "you should use the English plural."

121

"I'm hungry," said Lulu. "Should we go back and have lunch?"

"It's past lunchtime," Frankie said, but dove into the water. She swam to the dangling rope, grasped it, and hauled herself out of the pool. Water streamed from her clothes as she climbed hand over hand to the top.

"Show-off," Algie muttered.

"Octopuses," Frankie called as she disappeared through the cave opening.

Lulu rolled her eyes. "Being scared always makes her grumpy. She was terrified when we lost you earlier."

"I can't climb that rope," Algie said. "Not like that."

Lulu took lengths of cord from her rucksack and fashioned them into ascenders—stirrup-like loops on sliding knots that Algie could stand in to shimmy up the rope. Once he was safely at the top, Lulu climbed out the same way Frankie had.

Frankie sat on her equipment bag, picking burrs off her socks.

"Octopuses," she said.

"No wonder we didn't know this place existed." Lulu shook her head, staring at the clump of shrubs guarding the cave's opening. "You can't see it unless you're right on top. Algie, we found some of your things floating in the river. I think your asthma inhaler is all right, but your field notebook isn't." Alligator teeth had sunk halfway through the book, and the pages stuck together in a soggy mass.

Since Lulu was the lightest, Algie shared her waterbug for the journey home. It was difficult balancing two people on such a persnickety craft, and the inhaled swamp water had aggravated Algie's lungs. The harder he tried to suppress his coughs, the more his body shook.

"Can you try not to jiggle so much?" Lulu called over the whoosh of the fan.

The request was so unreasonable that Algie did not answer. The conversation he had overheard in the cave grated raw in his mind. He clenched his teeth and hung on.

CHAPTER

22

THAT NIGHT, ALGIE knelt by the fire in his room, peeling apart his notebook's waterlogged pages and holding them up to dry.

The door banged open, and Lulu tumbled in.

"Come quick," she gasped. "It's Professor Champion. He— he's caught something."

Frankie was waiting in the atrium. Without a word, the three children ran outside and across the starlit lawn. Palm trees nodded and whispered overhead, shivering in the breeze.

Down by the river dock, floodlights illuminated the *Flying Dancer* airship as it floated atop the water. The harsh artificial lighting drained the scene of color and gave every object multiple shadows.

A huge gray form swung from a winch on the *Flying Dancer*'s deck. Algie's stomach swung with it. When they reached the shadow of the overgrown stegosaurus bush at the foot of the lawn, they could finally see what dangled from that horrible hook.

It was Jasper the hammerhead shark. Blood trickled from his gills and made dark tears down his face. His eyes stared flat and sightless.

On the river dock stood Mr. Davenport in slippers and a pale blue dressing gown. He leaned his elbows against a piling, talking to Professor Champion.

"Here's the reward, and a tip for prompt service." He handed the professor a stack of bills. "This fellow will look smashing over the library mantelpiece, don't you think?"

"You can't have him." The professor pocketed the money. "I already have a buyer who collects this sort of thing, and they're less pinchpenny than you, Aloysius."

"But you caught him in my waters," Mr. Davenport protested.

"And I have a paper with your signature entitling me to the resale of any animal captured on your grounds. Paid good money for it too."

"Then give me that reward back!"

"No, no." The professor dodged Mr. Davenport's grab. "The shark was a nuisance, and you wanted it gone. I wish all my jobs were this easy. The brute came like a tame kitten."

Algie could take it no longer. He burst from the bushes.

"Jasper could have eaten me when he had the chance," he cried. "It wasn't his fault he thought I'd give him food."

"Now look here—" Mr. Davenport began, but Professor Champion cut him off.

"You mean he didn't eat you before I rescued you. What if he was less patient with the next rowboat he flipped? You forget I saw everything from above."

"Don't act like you care." Frankie arrived at Algie's side with Lulu close behind. "All you want is money. You'd be happy if Algie got eaten."

"It almost ate you too, Frankie," Mr. Davenport said. "I heard the whole story."

"You told on Jasper?" Lulu turned accusing eyes on Professor Champion.

"Certainly I did, little girl. Do you have any idea how many boaters and swimmers are out in that ocean on any given day? Of course, you do—you know perfectly well."

"You have a tranquilizer gun," Algie said. "You could have taken him somewhere away from people."

"Aren't you the boy who wants to become a naturalist? A real naturalist knows that hammerhead sharks can't breathe if they're not swimming."

Tears stung Algie's eyes. He shook them away.

"You should have stopped people from feeding him." Algie took a deep breath and looked at Mr. Davenport. "You should have taken better care of him."

Mr. Davenport sighed. "I agree it's a pity, especially if you children were fond of the animal. But frankly, I have more important things to do than babysit fifteen-foot-long man-eaters.

I'd feel irresponsible letting the creature roam at large after what happened. My guests' safety is my priority, and I don't enjoy the idea of my daughters being eaten either. I allow you children to take some risks, but this was getting out of control."

Algie wiped his eyes on his sleeve, furious at himself for appearing weak. Mr. Davenport's answer left him strangely hollow.

"If this gathering is over, I'll take my leave." Professor Champion put a foot on the *Dancer's* rope ladder. "I'll be back after dropping off the specimen, so hold my room, Aloysius."

He ascended the ladder, and the idling airship's hum increased to a roar. Dirt and leaves bit Algie's face as the *Dancer* rose into the air and pivoted.

Slowly, the great craft moved off.

Something fluttered behind the topiary stegosaurus.

"Madam Maximus?" asked Lulu.

Madam inched from behind the bush.

"I saw lights," she said. "I thought—is everything all right?"

"The professor is off on a business jaunt," said Mr. Davenport. "He'll be back soon, more's the pity."

"Where did he go?" Madam Maximus slapped a mosquito.

"Better ask him." Mr. Davenport proffered his arm. "You, children—back to bed, the lot of you."

"That's funny," Lulu whispered, as they trailed behind the adults. "Why would she be lurking behind that bush?"

"How can you think anything's funny at a time like this?" Frankie's eyes were blank and wide, as though they could not stop seeing Jasper's dripping blood. "I'd rather have twenty guests eaten than Jasper murdered because people can't do what they're told."

Miserable as he was, Algie could not let that pass.

"You shouldn't say that, Frankie," he said.

"Yes, I should," she flashed. "One animal is worth twenty of these pointless tourists. All they do is clutter up the beach."

"If you really think one animal worth twenty humans, would you have eaten bacon this morning?" Algie demanded. "Or is it just you who's so much better than everyone else?"

"So you're on Professor Champion's side again? You think Jasper deserved to die?"

"No!" It was difficult to argue when Algie was so confused himself. He hated Professor Champion's callousness, but in some ways the professor was right. Jasper's associating humans with food was dangerous. Keeping people safe was important. "But I hate it when you talk like that—like people are worthless if they don't matter to you personally."

"How can you make excuses for them? They're murderers— at least the ones who kept feeding him after we told them to stop."

"I'm not making excuses," Algie said. "There should be laws, or something, to keep it from happening. But just because someone makes bad or thoughtless decisions doesn't mean they should be shark food. I've done plenty of stupid things myself."

"I believe it." Frankie stuck her nose in the air.

"Lulu, back me up," said Algie. "I'm not the only person who thinks like this."

Lulu cast a frightened glance at Frankie and remained silent.

"All right," said Algie. He no longer cared whether Frankie kicked him off the crew. He was sick of being a pushover. "While we're on the subject, there's something else you'll want to shout at me about. We can't tell anyone about the octopi."

"If that's a joke, it's not funny!" Frankie halted, raising her voice until Lulu squeaked "Shhh!" and pointed at the adults.

"The most sensational discovery of the century," Frankie hissed. "A social, euryhaline species of giant octopus? This is our chance to prove to the scientific community—to the whole world—that we're naturalists with the best of them! And you want me to keep quiet about it?"

Algie squirmed, aware he was about to sound inexcusably priggish. "Don't you think some things are more important than recognition?"

"Without recognition you aren't anything," Frankie said. At the same time, Lulu asked "Like what?"

"Like protecting things that need it," Algie said.

Frankie's sandy eyelashes lowered, the way a bull's might when it was about to charge. "And you think a two-ton giant octopus needs protecting?"

"She's a nesting mother," Algie said. "And if they're escaping the red tide, her family is trapped here. With Professor Champion and your father." He clenched his jaw, remembering Jasper strung from the winch, his grace and power drained away with the blood on the polished deck.

Frankie's mouth tightened too. Her eyes were bright, as though she might cry.

"Don't you dare say a word about Papa," she said.

"You're telling me that if your father learns about an undiscovered species living on his grounds, he won't try to make a profit out of it?" Algie said. "And what about the professor? You heard him talking about that collector of his." He looked again to Lulu for backup; but though her eyes were anguished, her mouth stayed shut.

"Papa will understand that the octopuses need protection," Frankie said. "They're not like Jasper—not dangerous. We'll make him understand."

"Like you made him understand about those plume birds he sold to the professor." Algie shook his head. "Why is it wrong for Professor Champion to kill Jasper for safety reasons, and not wrong for you to put Octavia in danger because you want to be famous?"

Frankie's eyes sparked. "You're jealous! You want to convince us not to tell so you can spring the story by yourself."

"You don't believe that," Algie said. "If we wait for the red tide to clear up—"

"That could be months! And Professor Champion will discover her and steal our story—"

"I don't care!" Algie shouted. "This decision is about her life, not your ego!"

For a split second, he thought Frankie was going to punch him. Judging by her expression, she thought so too. Then she spun on her heel and walked off. Lulu hung her head and scuttled after her sister.

CHAPTER

23

THE NEXT MORNING, Algie tiptoed through the door joining his room to Everett's. A pajama-clad arm dangled from a snoring lump of covers.

"Everett," Algie whispered. His brother had been avoiding him, but Algie hoped time had cooled him off. He needed advice.

The lump snored louder.

"Everett!" Algie shook the lump and jumped back. Experience had taught him to stay out of range when his brother was rousted from sleep.

Everett sat up, bleary-eyed and bristling. "You'd better be here to tell me the hotel's on fire."

"Worse." Algie climbed onto the bed and crossed his legs. "I got in a fight with the Davenport girls."

"You should have given me a warning. I would have put money on them."

"It wasn't a fistfight." Algie scowled. "I said something Frankie—Francisca—didn't agree with, and she jumped all over me."

"Who does that sound like?"

"How long are you going to stay mad?" Algie demanded. "I'll say I'm sorry if you want. What more do you expect?"

"Why does it matter what I expect? After all, I'm a traitor who doesn't care about you."

Yanking the covers from beneath Algie, Everett disappeared into the bathroom and slammed the door. The sound of the running bathtub reverberated beneath.

Algie stared at the closed door, trying to remember their last conversation. Had he said that to Everett? Yes, but—he'd been angry.

You could have been nicer, said the voice in his head that forced him to face things he rather wouldn't. *You didn't have to say it like that.*

Algie considered. Arguing with Frankie last night had given him perspective on how Everett might have felt when Algie attacked him. Yes, they disagreed over Professor Champion's plume-hunting. But no matter what either of them said to the contrary, Algie knew his brother cared about him. He'd said what was untrue to try to hurt Everett. Well, it had worked. A wash of unhappiness engulfed him.

Everett's voice issued with a cloud of steam beneath the bathroom door.

"Aside from fighting with the Davenports, are you staying out of trouble like I told you to?"

Algie thought of almost drowning in the alligator's jaws yesterday. Sure, Everett cared about him—but not enough to spend time with him. He left the room without answering.

Stomping back into his own room, Algie yanked on his day clothes and jerked open the hall door. He fell over Frankie sitting in front of it.

"I'm sorry for last night." She snapped her book shut. "I knew you were right, but it was easier to get mad at you. And you were right that my theory about Professor Champion letting loose a monster was a bunch of hogwash."

"Excuse me?" Algie tried to wrap his mind around this new situation.

"I already apologized. Don't make me do it again. Here, I brought you this."

She handed him a leather explorer's rucksack, bristling with straps and buckles.

Algie took it in astonishment. The leather was new and scratch-free. Inside was a waxed canvas dry bag, a field notebook with attached waterproof pencil, and a heavy brass cylinder.

"You're giving me your flashlight?" He hefted it in his hand.

"This one's better than mine. It works underwater." Frankie's crooked smile was sunny and confident.

But despite the gleaming equipment, resentment squeezed Algie's heart. Did she believe expensive gifts would make up for everything? How spineless did she think him?

133

A slammed door echoed in his mind. He had gone to Everett wanting to fix things, and his brother had shut him out. It felt terrible realizing that Everett no longer believed in him. If he did, he would have faith that Algie could right their relationship.

Algie lifted his eyes to Frankie's. The situation with Everett was too painful to touch, but here in front of him was something he could fix. Not speaking up when Frankie was rude or unfair counted as being a pushover. Believing the best in people did NOT make him a pushover.

"You look funny," Frankie said. "Open the book!"

The stiff bindings squeaked as Algie lifted the cover. Tucked between blank pages was the photograph from the cave. The image of himself was uninspiring. He looked like what he was—a waterlogged schoolboy. But beside him . . .

Shivers of awe crawled up Algie's arms as he gazed at the *Octopus giganteus*. How long were her arms? Forty, fifty feet? Her mantle would have grazed his hotel room's arched ceiling. But the black-and-white picture did not do her justice. It could never capture her powerful grace, her living iridescence.

"The lighting was too poor in the other photos." Frankie tilted her head, admiring her own handiwork. "You couldn't tell what you were looking at. But once the red tide clears up, this will be on the front page of every newspaper in the country."

"Thanks, Francisca," Algie said.

"Shut up. I should have told you to call me Frankie ages ago." She kicked at the carpet. "When I met you, I said I wouldn't slow down for anyone. I know I've been hard on you, but . . . well, I guess I forgot that a good naturalist knows not to go fast all the time. If you do, you can miss things that are important."

Algie thought of those long Chicago days stuck coughing in bed, nothing to look at but pigeons and squirrels outside his window. At the time, he'd wished to be anywhere else, but those days had laid the foundation for his love for nature. They'd taught him patience, stillness, and appreciation.

"You're right," he said. "Thanks."

Frankie stuck out her hand. "Friends?"

Algie shook it.

"Sure," he said. "Frankie."

Frankie flashed her grin again, and Algie grinned back.

★

At breakfast, Algie sat with the Davenports instead of his own family. Mrs. Emsworth waved at him, surrounded by a circle of her own new friends. Out of the corner of his eye, Algie saw Everett wolf down his food and then stalk from the solarium.

After breakfast, the children collected their equipment and headed to the boathouse. A line of people in traveling clothes blocked the atrium, waiting for O'Conner at the manager's desk.

"More people leaving?" Frankie groaned. "I thought the squeamish ones had gone!"

"*Shh!*" Lulu held up a hand.

"Is it true the Paraíso guarantees one genuine spook-sighting per booking?" asked a thin, bespectacled man. A finger marked his place in a copy of *The Horrible Haunting of Haleyford Hall*.

"Well . . . " O'Conner cleared his throat. "Not *guarantee*, as it were . . . but under the present state of affairs, I can hint that it's highly likely!"

"They're horror tourists!" Lulu bounced with elation. "That's what's popular right now—being scared! Maybe the hotel will stay open after all!"

"Off for a soak in the sulfur baths?" Mrs. Emsworth trotted up, her lace sunshade over her shoulder. "Everett told me your plans for the morning. So healthful! I may take a dip myself— after our Swamp Spook walk, that is." She linked arms with Mrs. Pliskett and swept off, their feathery hats swaying.

Frankie stared at Algie. "Did you tell your family we were going to dip our toes alongside all the hoity-toity tourists with gout?"

"No!" Algie yelped. "At least—" He'd been so taken aback that he hadn't contradicted his mother. Did that count as lying? What did Everett think he was playing at, trapping Algie into deceit!

He was reminding Algie of his hold over him, that's what. The threat was clear. *Leave me alone and I'll keep Mother off your back.* Algie scowled.

"Would your mother let you come with us if she knew what you were doing?" Lulu asked.

"I don't know." Algie felt miserable. Mrs. Emsworth had said he could run around and get stronger. But he hadn't asked permission to befriend swamp monsters. "Does your dad know about your zipping around the swamp, stalking wild animals?"

"Oh, yes," Frankie said. "He likes us to learn how to manage risk. Says it's good for the character."

"Within reason," Lulu added.

"There's sulfur in all these springs," Frankie added, "so you're technically not lying. Come on, Algie."

★

Since Algie's waterbug was at the bottom of the bayou, they journeyed through the swamp in a pirogue—a flat-bottomed boat with a single paddle, designed for shallow water. Algie was relieved. The thought of braving a waterbug again made his breakfast roll over in his stomach.

At the octopi's den, the girls knotted their rope around a palm trunk and slid down into the water. Bubbles simmered around them, gleaming in the shaft of radiance.

"Jump," Lulu called. "It's plenty deep."

The pool shelved downward toward a yawning crevice, where sand whirled endlessly from some bottomless wellspring. The gleaming water looked sinister. What was different? He had gone to bed feeling all right, but today he was afraid.

Yesterday Algie had almost drowned in an alligator's jaws. Yesterday he'd thought Everett would forgive him. And yesterday Professor Champion had killed yet another animal that Algie and the girls had been unable to protect.

Today was different. Because today Algie knew how much he could get hurt.

He shut his eyes and jumped. A swooping drop, and he sliced into the water.

Down, down. Too far down. That gaping hole would suck him in. Algie paddled frantically, his heart swelling. Had he forgotten how to swim? Was he stuck in a deadly undercurrent?

Kick with the legs, sweep with the arms. Algie kicked and swept and the water obeyed, buoying him to the surface. Gasping, he swam to the ledge.

Pulpy sidled over and began to rummage through his knapsack. His spirits lifting at the octopus's friendliness, Algie picked him up and took a deep breath, calming his heartrate. They had discovered a magnificent new species. The octopi were trusting; they could observe them at will. Discovery was unlikely in this labyrinthine swamp.

It would be all right. This was going to be a wonderful winter.

He kept his gaze turned away from the sunken bones and unnerving crevice.

CHAPTER

24

IN THE WEEKS that followed, the children visited the cave almost every day. The octopi seemed to enjoy the company and settle into their new home.

One morning in late February, they were lounging a mile or so from the cave. Octavia had taken her family on an outing to one of the nearby small springs, and Lulu was playing with the babies in the water. Though not underground, the pool was nearly as protected as the cave. Trees walled it around, curtained with Spanish moss.

Frankie and Algie sat on the bank, surrounded by notes weighted down with stones.

"Here, Thursday," Algie called, snapping his fingers at one of the octopi who was escaping with his pen. "Bring that back!"

"I think that's Tuesday," Frankie said. For simplicity's sake, they had named the other juveniles after the days of the week. Unfortunately, there was nothing simple about telling seven restless octopi apart. If they stayed still long enough and didn't change colors, Algie could see the differences between their at-rest patterns of spots; but that only occurred once in a blue moon.

"Still no sign of the red tide clearing up." Frankie propped her elbows on her knees. "At least it's keeping the horror tourists happy."

"Hush," Algie said. He was watching Pulpy, who had climbed onto a rock. Insects hummed, leaves rustled—the typical noises of the swamp.

"I think we should hide," Algie said.

"Why?" asked Frankie. But she kept her voice low.

"Look at Pulpy," said Algie. "That's his 'danger' posture."

Alerted by Pulpy's stillness, the other octopi stopped frolicking. One by one, they changed color and disappeared among roots and rocks. Octavia sank to the bottom of the pool, spread her mantle, and vanished.

Algie craned his neck. He could see nothing in the pool except sand and sunken leaves.

Lulu exited the water and scrambled up a cabbage palm, while Algie and Frankie stuffed papers into their knapsacks.

"Over there." Frankie nodded toward a clump of saw palmetto. She and Algie flung themselves flat and wormed beneath the fan-shaped leaves. Toothed leafstalks raked Algie's arms, and dirt gritted between his teeth as he squirmed into position. Through a gap in the fronds, he could see the pool's surface.

A curtain of hanging moss parted and Professor Champion paddled into the spring. He stood upright in a pirogue, eyes glinting beneath his safari helmet. His giant tranquilizer gun was slung over one shoulder. Algie had heard him boast of halting a charging hippo with that gun.

Algie held his breath as the pirogue slipped farther into the pool. Could Octavia fool the professor's experienced eyes? She lay right beneath him, shielded by nothing but ten feet of clear water.

The professor reminded Algie of a stalking heron — slow and efficient, ready to spring into blinding action when he spotted his prey. His gaze swept the clearing and landed on a spot by their hiding place.

Frankie pinched Algie and jerked her chin toward the pool. Algie's hands went numb with horror. His field notebook lay on the bank! The notebook with the photograph of Octavia.

CHAPTER

25

PAIN SEARED THROUGH Algie's ankle. Fire ants! Beside him, Frankie bit her fist. The ants must be attacking her too. But they could not move. The smallest crackle would give them away. He could not tell if Professor Champion had spotted the notebook, or merely some other sign of their presence—a careless footprint or flattened clump of grass. If the professor stepped onto the bank, there was no question that he would see the book.

The pirogue nosed against the mud. Algie gave the game up for lost.

As Professor Champion moved to step out of the boat, a jet of water shot from the reeds. It hit the professor in the face.

"Ouch!" Taken by surprise, the professor lost his balance. His feet shot from under him, and he slammed onto his back in the bottom of the boat.

Octavia acted. Her yellow eyes glowed from the depths as she reached up and curled one powerful arm around the stern of the boat. Professor Champion was dumped into the water. He surfaced to an empty pool, littered by a floating mess of match-wood.

White-faced, Professor Champion swam to the side and climbed onto an overhanging branch. It was the first time Algie had seen him shaken. He peered into the depths of the spring, then around at the trees and the splintered wreckage of his boat. The entire episode had taken less than ten seconds.

The professor took a flare pistol from his belt and fired it into the air. An umbrella of white sparks burst above the trees.

In answer, a droning hum roared out overhead. The *Flying Dancer* soared into view.

Algie took advantage of the noise to swat ants from his legs, his eyes watering with pain. But he was worried. How long had the *Dancer* been lurking with its engine off? Who was piloting?

A shout drifted from the airship. Twisting onto his back, Algie squinted through the palmetto leaves.

Everett's face appeared over the *Dancer*'s railing.

Though he'd tried to steel himself for the possibility, the sight punched Algie in the gut. He rolled back around, hoping the girls wouldn't notice.

"Lower away," Professor Champion called.

"Aye-aye, sir!" Everett shouted back. A rope ladder unfurled from the *Dancer*. Professor Champion stepped onto it and took one last look around the glen.

"I know you brats are behind this," he said to the swamp at large. "And I'll find out what you're hiding, mark my words." He shook his fist, then grabbed the ladder as the airship lurched and bore him off over the trees.

As soon as the hum faded, Algie and Frankie clawed their way out of the palmetto and raced to plunge their legs in the water. Angry red and white welts dotted Algie's skin from his ankles to his knees. He ripped off his shoes and socks, brushing away the balled-up ants.

Lulu dropped from her tree as Octavia peeked above the water. Eight babies returned to their normal coloring and jetted through the debris toward their mother. To no one's surprise, Pulpy appeared on the bank that had assaulted Professor Champion.

"That's one for the notebooks." Lulu's voice shook. "I knew the octopuses were smart, but I didn't know they were that smart."

"They know a thug when they see one." Frankie swished her feet through the water. "Algie, was that your brother up there?"

Algie's eyes felt hot. "I asked him to stay away from the professor, but he wouldn't listen. All he cares about is getting to fly the airship." What if Frankie thought he'd told Everett about the octopuses and where to look for them?

Frankie picked a piece of waterweed out of the pool and examined a tiny snail crawling over it.

"Don't feel too bad," she said. "We can't always help what our family does."

"We feel the same way about Papa," Lulu added. "We love him, but he's so stubborn."

Algie managed a small smile. Everett's choice of allegiance stung, but it was nice that the sisters wanted to comfort him.

"By the way," Frankie said, with a stern return to her captain's voice, "what possessed you to leave that book out?"

"I was in a hurry," Algie groaned. He gestured at his swollen ant bites. "Please, can we agree I've already been punished?"

Collecting her brood, Octavia oozed out of the spring and disappeared into the network of backwaters leading to her den.

"She's got the right idea," Frankie said. "Let's get out of here. We should have known things were too peaceful to last."

★

"Wait up, Algie!

Everett was on his way back from the golf course, carrying a bag of clubs. He waved goodbye to Angel O'Dare and Parker James, then jogged through the coconut grove toward Algie.

Algie groaned. He felt less prepared than usual for a clash. After the morning's misadventure with Professor Champion, they had taken the *Diving Belle* downriver and out into the ocean for the afternoon, keeping away from the inland bayous and Octavia's grotto in case the professor tried to follow. His throat stung from breathing the red-tide air and the stench of beach carcasses. His eyes ached with squinting through the microscope in the *Belle*'s dim laboratory.

Frankie and Lulu looked at Algie, then at Everett jouncing up with his golf bag and jaunty cap.

"Want us to stay?" Frankie asked. "We'll back you up. Take him out at the knees with a putter if he's bothering you."

"Thanks," Algie said. "I'll handle it."

The girls scampered off through the topiary. Algie watched them go. Though the sisters did not always get along, they stuck together, even through fights—instead of ignoring each other the way Everett had ignored Algie for the past month. Granted, Algie had done nothing to bridge the gap.

"I saw you in the swimming pool yesterday." Everett swung into step beside Algie. "You've come a long way since we arrived."

No thanks to you. Algie bit the words back.

"You're in a good mood," he said instead.

"I won our golf match. Were those the Davenport girls with you?"

"Yes."

"Mother's not keeping the leash too tight? I've been running interference for you."

Algie did not smile back. He didn't enjoy feeling like he was deceiving their mother. He had been through some sticky situations with the Davenports, though they always escaped without too many scratches. His mother wanted him safe, but he was getting stronger . . . surely that was safer than wasting his muscles and lungs away in his bedroom.

Probably he should discuss these tradeoffs with Mrs. Emsworth. But if he did, she might disagree. Algie wished Everett would go away and stop bringing up unwanted topics.

"Speaking of Mother," Everett said, in response to Algie's silence, "what do you think about everything she's been up to?"

"I don't know what to think," Algie said. For the first time since he could remember, his mother was caught up in activities that did not revolve around him. The horror fad was still in full swing. When Algie had risen that morning, she had been fast asleep, worn out after a midnight "ghost hike" to the beach. Thankfully, the octopi had kept away from the hotel since the circus performance incident.

"Looks like one of the aerialists forgot their practice line." Everett nodded at a low rope stretched between two palms. He set down his golf clubs, stepped onto the line, and steadied his back against a trunk. Clumsily, but without falling, he walked from one end to the other.

"Impressed?" He hopped down.

Algie was, though he wouldn't admit it. "Did Angel teach you that?" he asked.

"She did. There isn't anyone like her in the world." Everett's eyes grew starry, but he recollected himself and held out his elbow. Algie grasped it and climbed onto the tightrope.

"What are you up to these days?" Everett asked. "Besides swimming, I mean. I hardly see you at meals."

We saw you *this morning.* Algie swallowed those words too. Another yelling match with Everett would accomplish nothing. His brother was trying to be nice.

"A lot of research," he said, and took a step. His mind went back to the seawater samples they had collected that afternoon. His asthma had been under control all morning in the swamps— in fact, some days he was almost sure his lungs were improving— but, as always, the moment they neared the beach, his nose began to burn and his chest to squeeze. Though he'd stayed out of the water with a bandanna tied over his mouth and nose, he had still ended up needing his rescue inhaler this afternoon, and their expedition had been cut short. Frustration at his own body pricked him again. The line wobbled. He grabbed Everett's head for balance.

"Ouch! Don't yank my ears off!" Everett snapped. Recovering, he asked, in his former friendly tone, "Any closer to that fabulous scientific discovery you set out to make?"

Alarm bells jangled in Algie's mind.

"We're looking for the cause of red tide," he said. "Are you interested in microbiology?"

"What about this 'mystery beast' everyone's talking about?" Everett's voice was too carefully careless. "Have you seen anything strange in the swamps?"

Algie let go of Everett and jumped off so that the tightrope stretched between them. The ground jarred his feet. "Did Professor Champion tell you to ask me that?"

Everett had the grace to flush.

"He's not the complete ruffian you think he is. I don't agree with some of his methods, but he's done a lot to make science and natural history accessible to the public. He was the one who told me to make sure Mother gave you the chance to get out and explore on your own. And he's an excellent teacher. This morning he let me pilot his airship—"

"You mean he bribed you to spy on me." Anger pounded Algie's throat. "He's using you to try and get us to lead him to—"

Algie stopped short. He'd almost told Everett about Octavia!

The slip was lost on Everett. Though he'd been starry-eyed when he mentioned Angel, he glowed almost golden when he spoke of the airship.

"The *Flying Dancer* is a perfect name for her," he sighed. "When you're behind the helm, you feel like she's alive—"

"How long have you been sneaking around after us?"

Everett's dreaminess vanished.

"This is why it's impossible to talk to you." He gripped the tightrope so hard that white dots appeared over his knuckles. "You already know everything, so I guess it's pointless for you to listen—to *me*, anyway. Did you ever think I might be worried about you?"

"About me?" Algie asked, completely wrong-footed. "Why?"

"Oh, I don't know—maybe because you're running around in the swamp after some wild unidentified beast? Professor Champion is worried too. He's seen enough to know that this creature is huge and potentially dangerous—and though he isn't a saint, he's a first-rate naturalist. A lot of people are treating this like a game. They shouldn't. If you kids are messing with this animal, you're in over your heads."

Algie was stunned. It never occurred to him that Everett could have a motive for prying, other than desire to stay on Professor Champion's good side and get his hands on the airship. Dazed, he collected his defenses.

"Frankie and Lulu grew up here," he said. "They know what they're doing."

Everett snorted. "Professor Champion says those kids wouldn't know their own limitations if they ran them over in a motorcar."

The shot hit too close to home. Algie already felt uncomfortable enough about the risks they were running. His temper flamed.

"What are you going to do? Tell Mother I'm too incompetent to be trusted and ask her to ship me home?"

"I haven't decided yet," said Everett. "But this isn't a joke, Algie. If you kids aren't careful, someone's going to get hurt."

CHAPTER

26

ALGIE WOKE BEFORE dawn. The conversation with Everett hung over him like a bad feeling after a nightmare. He opened his window and leaned out. Cool, salty air filled his lungs. The gravel path seemed to shine in the dimness.

On the far side of the lawn, something glimmered. Lights like enormous fireflies, swirling toward the greenhouse.

Algie dressed, went downstairs, and ran barefoot through the grass. He paused to put his shoes on before entering the greenhouse.

Octavia lounged in the Fountain of Youth. She rolled a yellow eye as Algie sat down at the edge of the fountain.

"I won't bother you," he said. "Do you sneak in here to relax on your own? I know what it's like to need a break from your family."

But Algie sighed. As much as he told himself he didn't miss Everett, the friction between them was like a blister that wouldn't heal. Even his own mother seemed to have lost interest in him. Was there no happy medium between her fussing over his every twitch and forgetting his existence?

"But I can't let Everett tell her about you," Algie said to Octavia. He had no doubt that if his mother grew worried, she would spin straight back to the first extreme.

Octavia swirled. Algie brushed his fingers through the water and thought of the statue of the mother in the octopi's den. It belonged there with Octavia, the embodiment of everything strong and nurturing. Would his own mother have yanked an alligator off his back? Or would she just have screamed and gone into hysterics?

"We took the *Diving Belle* out yesterday," he said. "I got some seawater samples. We're trying to figure out what causes the red tide." His mind ran for the thousandth time over the funny, reddish-brown blobs tumbling under his microscope in every one of their samples. Could they be the key to the dead marine animals? If only he had some healthy seawater for comparison. He imagined soaring in the *Flying Dancer*, taking samples all along the Gulf.

A branch snapped behind them. Algie whirled. A clump of fan palms quivered in the breathless air.

"Who's that?" Algie called.

No one answered. He checked behind the palms. No one.

"Probably a macaque," he said, but he was uncertain.

Octavia crawled from the fountain and lumbered away to her secret back exit. Even in the midst of his unease, Algie marveled at how she could squeeze her enormous bulk unharmed through the broken pane of glass. When her last arm vanished, he returned to the spot behind the fan palms.

A gleam caught his eye. Algie licked his finger and touched it to the ground. He straightened up, holding a glittering gold sequin.

★

"Miss O'Dare!"

A sparkling procession of bleary-eyed acrobats trudged through the wet grass toward the swimming hall. The last figure turned at Algie's shout.

"Were you in the greenhouse a minute ago?" Algie fell into step beside Angel. With a twinge of surprise, he realized he was not puffing like he would have done a few weeks ago. He had run all the way across the grounds.

Angel's reaction surprised him. A flush reddened her cheeks.

"Were you?" she asked.

"Didn't you see me?" Algie asked, startled.

"No." Angel scowled.

"Did you see—anyone else?" *Like a giant octopus?* Now Algie was confused.

"I don't have time for this, kid," Angel snapped. "What's it to you?"

Algie put all his cards on the table. "Miss O'Dare, if you were in there and you did see—anyone—please don't mention it, all right? I know it may not seem important to you, but there's someone who could get hurt if people knew."

"Are you going to tell?" Angel asked.

"Of course not." Algie looked at her warily. "What are we talking about?"

"I'll keep my mouth shut if you do." Hoisting her equipment bag higher on her shoulder, Angel sprang up the steps to the swim hall.

Frowning, Algie watched the acrobats until Madam Maximus shut the double doors. He walked back up the lawn.

Lulu lay on her stomach beneath an oleander, squinting through a magnifying glass.

"This earthworm got rid of its tail," she said. "It was injured, and he wriggled it right off and went into his hole. Wouldn't it be nice if we could discard and regenerate our body parts that didn't work properly? You could have a new set of lungs. I'm not sure how you'd breathe while you were growing them back, though."

"We have bigger problems." Algie related his story.

"Angel spotted you with Octavia?" Lulu tapped her magnifying glass against her teeth. "That's not good."

"She promised not to tell," Algie said. "I don't know if we can trust her."

"Never trust anyone without good reason," Lulu advised. "Blackmail is easier. Let's go find Frankie and see what kind of dirt we can dig up."

154

Frankie was not in the breakfast room yet, so Algie and Lulu sat down to eat. But Algie could not calm his mind. He drained his orange juice, and then spotted Frankie in the doorway. One look at her face and he knew there was trouble.

As Algie and Lulu jumped up, Mrs. Emsworth rustled over.

"Have you heard the news? The professor is holding a lecture tonight—he says he's captured a creature unknown to science!" She waved to Lady Plumworthy. "Amelia, have you heard?"

"Frankie, what's going on?" Lulu gasped as they fled to the door. "The professor can't have Octavia. Algie saw her in the greenhouse!"

"I was coming to find you," Frankie moaned. "I heard him talking to Mrs. Emsworth. Octavia probably crawled right into his clutches!"

"Are we sure it's Octavia?" Algie demanded.

"'A creature unknown to science'—that's the phrase he used." Frankie raked her hands through her hair.

"We have to stay calm," Algie said, trying to convince himself as much as either of them. "If Octavia's at the cave, we don't have to worry. Let me get my gear and I'll be back in five minutes."

He tore up the staircase and burst into his room. His knapsack lay on the bed. Remembering the downfalls of over-hurrying, Algie pawed through the bag to check his equipment. Canteen, first aid kit, asthma inhaler . . . where was his notebook? The notebook with the photo of Octavia . . .

Algie dug through the bag again, and then dumped the gear on the floor. A rummage through drawers proved fruitless, and a scouring of bedclothes. He even crawled under the bed. The book wasn't there.

Sneezing, Algie backed out from beneath the bed. A waft of warm air hit his face.

His window stood ajar. He knew he had shut it before leaving the room—he remembered wrestling with the stiff, humidity-swollen sash. But he had not thought to lock it.

Algie knew only one person capable of strolling through a third-story window.

CHAPTER

27

FRANKIE WAS DISPATCHED to the octopi's den while Algie and Lulu re-ransacked the room. When Frankie returned, she looked worried.

"Octavia wasn't there. Neither was Pulpy. Don't panic—they've been out fishing when we've visited before, and it didn't mean a calamity. The other babies were upset that I didn't stay. They wanted me to play with them."

Algie scanned her face. "Something else happened."

"Yes . . . and no. I took the pirogue so no one could follow my noise. And no one did follow. I made sure of that. But," she shivered, "the whole time I couldn't shake the feeling of someone watching. I was almost too scared to rappel down into the cave. I kept imagining Angel swinging through the trees and untying my rope."

"If she's got that photograph, it's only a matter of time before she tells," Lulu said. "Think how much it could be worth."

"The notebook is worse than the photo," Frankie said. "What if she gives it to the professor?"

"Don't," Algie groaned. The thought of his hard work being appropriated by Professor Champion was agonizing. He kept everything in that notebook: measurements, feeding patterns, behaviors, personality traits.

"You don't think—" Lulu glanced at the door leading to Everett's room.

"No," Algie said. "Everett couldn't have taken it, because I keep that door locked."

A squeaking emanated from the bathroom. It sounded like fingers rubbing over metal. Algie was relieved when Pulpy oozed from the bathtub faucet.

"At least you're safe." He lifted the octopus to his shoulder, then unfurled his spyglass and pointed it out the window. The *Flying Dancer* floated on the water beside the boathouse. Professor Champion was nowhere to be seen, but two burly figures lounged on deck with cowboy hats shading their eyes.

"Any chance we can board her and see what he's hiding?" Shouldering into the window beside Algie, Frankie grabbed the spyglass. "Oh no—he's got Gabe and Lenny on the job."

"He set a guard?" Lulu pushed between them. "Why?"

Frankie snapped her fingers. "I remember now! He said someone broke into his airship. I was so upset about Octavia, I forgot."

Algie remembered the security guards they had met on the beach his first day on the *Diving Belle*.

"Aren't they your friends?" he asked. "Maybe they can help us."

Lulu shook her head. "They're like bulldogs. When they take a job, they take it seriously. Algie, isn't there *anywhere* else that book might be?"

Algie unstuck one of Pulpy's arms from around his neck.

"Actually," he said, "I do have one more idea."

★

They crept through the halls. When they reached Angel's room on the fifth floor, Algie whipped Pulpy from his backpack and held him up to the lock. Always willing to investigate shiny objects, Pulpy fiddled away while Algie scanned the empty passage on tenterhooks of suspense.

Finally, the door clicked open.

Frankie's eyes widened. "I can't believe that worked."

"I told you he could do it!" Algie stashed Pulpy in his knapsack, turned the handle, and stepped into Angel's room.

The space was more spartan than the other rooms Algie had seen at the Hotel Paraíso. Excess cushions and rugs had been removed. A thin Japanese-style sleeping mat lay on the floor beside the bed. No other personal belongings were visible.

"Where do you think she hid the book?" Lulu whispered.

Algie pulled open a drawer, and a photograph fluttered out—

Angel, Everett, and Parker James in golf attire. As usual, Angel's smile looked ironic, as though she were laughing at some secret joke on her.

"Looking for something?" inquired a deep voice behind them.

★

"Found them prying in Miss Angel's room," was the strongman's verdict as he delivered the three to Mr. Davenport's office. "I don't know how they picked the lock, but it's not a skill I like to see in youngsters."

"Breaking and entering?" Mr. Davenport looked up from a stack of papers. "That deserves a lecture—preferably a long and boring one. Hubert," addressing the strongman, "is there any chance you could deliver several hours of strong remarks on the morality of rifling through other people's belongings?"

"No," said Hubert.

Mr. Davenport looked disappointed. "I can't either. I have a business trip to prepare for. Well, I suppose a penalty will do."

"Do you mean you're punishing us?" Frankie asked.

"Of course not," said Mr. Davenport. "Only demonstrating that actions have consequences. Hubert, do you think Madam Maximus could spare you this afternoon?"

Hubert's eyebrows shot up and he began to back away. Mr. Davenport smirked. Algie gulped.

CHAPTER

28

*"**THE TENANT OF** Wildfell Hall*, by Acton Bell." Frankie jotted down the name, dropped her forehead against the shelf, and groaned. "Do you think Papa really needs a list of every book in the library?"

"At least you're dry." Lulu brandished a mop, dribbling suds over her already soaked skirt. "Do you think we can overpower him? It's almost time for Professor Champion's lecture."

Algie glanced at the bull-like shoulders of Hubert the strongman, distorted by the stained-glass panels of the door outside which he stood guard.

"Not a chance." He adjusted the handkerchief keeping dust out of his nose and mouth. "Where's Pulpy?"

"He was in my clean bucket a minute ago," Lulu said.

"You don't think he could have gotten up the chimney?"

"I wouldn't put anything past that octopus," Frankie said. "I'm sure he's fine."

Algie could not be so calm. Apart from Pulpy's inability to stay put, here they were dusting books and mopping floors while Octavia might be languishing in some horrible cage of the professor's. But although he could never entirely share the Davenports' refusal to worry about things beyond their control, Algie knew it was a quality he should at least occasionally try to imitate. After all, Octavia was not defenseless.

Shoving away the feeling of impending doom, he swept his feather duster across one of the glass display cases lining the room. Beneath the glass, a book stood open on a stand. The pages were dirty and water-stained, yellow with age. The left-hand page showed several sketches of a machine similar to the waterbug Algie had crashed on his first venture into the swamp. The right-hand page contained a full-color illustration of the most bizarre outfit Algie had ever seen.

The caption was in Spanish, but he could tell by the pen-and-ink fish hovering about that it was a diving suit. It looked like a suit of armor designed for some strangely proportioned monster. Dozens of small circular viewports studded the helmet so the wearer could turn their head inside to see in any direction. The joints bulged, constructed of overlapping metal plates.

"Is this a design by the inventress you told me about?" he asked Lulu.

She came to look over his shoulder. "That's the Señora's diving suit. She actually built that one."

"A workable diving suit in the 1700s?" Now Algie was even more interested.

"I don't know if you could call it 'workable.'" Lulu wiped hair out of her eyes with her wrist. "It worked in her shallow dives, but she took it into the headspring one day and never came back."

"Did they ever find the suit?"

"No."

"We used to go searching for it," Frankie said from her ladder. "Think how impressive it would look in our study."

Algie shivered at the thought of those empty glass eyes reading over his shoulder. Before he could move to the next display case, the library doors opened.

"Mr. Davenport said you could come out at ten to seven," said the strongman. "If you head straight there, you'll be able to make that talk of the professor's. I'm headed that way myself."

The entire hotel seemed headed that way. Algie, Frankie, and Lulu navigated the crush outside the lecture room by crawling on their hands and knees through the crowd. Algie's cloud of doom redescended when he saw the curtain-draped rectangle dominating the stage: clearly the drapes covered some enormous tank or cage. The occupant of the cage made no noise. They would not know what was trapped inside until the professor chose to reveal it.

A few seats were open toward the back of the room. Algie sat down on the edge of a red plush cushion, curling and uncurling his toes inside his boots.

"What if it's Octavia?" Lulu whispered. She looked as nervous as Algie felt. Only Frankie sat with folded arms and composed mouth. Looking at her, Algie relaxed. Frankie might be stubborn and opinionated, but she was also capable and resourceful. No fight could be hopeless with Frankie on one's side.

A wave of lavender assaulted Algie's nose as his mother took the chair to his right. She wafted the air with her fan, her eyes bright and animated.

"I worried we wouldn't make it in time," she whispered. "I can't wait to see what the professor has in store for us!"

"Where were you?" Algie asked.

"On an excursion to the Spanish ruins down the coast. So deliciously spooky!" Settling her skirts, Mrs. Emsworth hoisted her spectacles to survey the audience. "What an unusual hat Mrs. Pliskett is wearing. Appropriate for the seaside, but a little too singular, don't you think?"

Three rows ahead, Mrs. Pliskett's top-heavy chapeau nodded above the crowd. There, reposing on a nest of ribbons, cheek-to-mantle with a stuffed kingfisher, was a baby *Octopus giganteus*. It had colored itself bright blue to match the hat and seemed proud of the result.

Algie and Lulu exchanged horrified glances.

On the other side of Lulu, Frankie sucked in her breath. Algie followed her gaze. A pair of soulful, horizontally barred eyes caught his and withdrew beneath the gown of the lady in front of him.

164

"Which one was that?" Lulu whispered.

"I couldn't tell," Algie whispered back. "I think Sunday is the one in the hat."

"Wednesday," Frankie hissed. "Get down!" This octopus was doing a passable imitation of a marble bust atop a cabinet, squashed between the motionless white heads of Ponce de Leon and William Bartram.

"They're all here," Lulu groaned. "What are we going to do?" Every corner of the room seemed to be full of wriggling arms and curious eyes. Algie could not believe the other guests hadn't noticed. It was only a matter of time.

Professor Champion took the stage, and the chatter hushed.

CHAPTER

29

"LADIES AND GENTLEMEN," said Professor Champion. "Tonight you have been granted the great privilege of being among the first to view an animal previously thought to be legendary. It is a testament to my skill as an outdoorsman that I was able to capture this glorious specimen unharmed."

Algie did not hear the rest. His attention was riveted by a lump wriggling along beneath the drapes. A lump the exact size and wriggliness of a baby Octopus giganteus.

Professor Champion's voice drawled back into his ears. "Without further ado, I present—" He released the drapes, and the green velvet cascaded to the ground.

Relief flooded Algie.

The crowd murmured in polite puzzlement. Professor

Champion did not seem to notice the anticlimax. He stood back, beaming with pride. The cage held a large panther, which surveyed the room with irritated twitches of its tail.

Frankie gasped.

"What is it?" Algie asked.

"A melanistic Florida panther."

"A what?"

"A black Florida panther! Nobody's ever documented one. But I think the guests were hoping for a more spectacular monster."

"Oh." Algie looked at the cat with renewed interest. Then he noticed the lump clinging to the cage door. Pulpy was doing his best to look like a decorative piece of ironwork, but Algie knew better.

Professor Champion droned on in a self-congratulatory monologue. Taking advantage of his preoccupation, Pulpy extended a stealthy tendril toward the lock. Not stealthy enough—the crowd perked up. Professor Champion looked over, too late. The cage door swung open, and Pulpy dove for cover.

With one liquid motion, the melanistic panther bounded through the air and landed noiselessly onstage. Professor Champion shouted and sprang forward, but Frankie sprang faster. She vaulted her chair, sprinted to the back of the room, and flung open the door.

The panther took off, streaking for the exit. Before the shocked audience could move, it was up the aisle and through the door. Frankie, Algie, and Lulu bolted after it.

"It might get lost in the hotel," Frankie shouted. "We have to make sure it gets out!"

The panther paused in the hall, then dashed into the Hibiscus Parlor. Seeing no outlet, it darted under a table as shrieks and screeches poured from the lecture hall behind. The big cat's paws made no sound on the carpet. Its ribs heaved in and out, the curved fangs visible as it panted with stress.

"Be careful," Algie called, but Frankie ran across the room and threw open the French doors leading to the patio. She doubled back to Algie and Lulu, hugging the wall to give the panther space.

"Yell!" she shouted, and Algie and Lulu raised their voices in a chorus of encouragement. The terrified panther shot out the door, leaping over a lumpy object draped across the flagstones. Its paws left wet, dark prints as it raced across the patio and disappeared into shadow.

"Chew on that, Professor!" Frankie crowed. She turned to leave, but Algie grabbed her arm, his eyes on the object outside the window.

"Let go." Frankie pulled herself free. "I want to see the prof's reaction."

"Wait a minute." Algie said. He crossed the parlor and looked out.

Madam Maximus lay crumpled in a heap, like the carcasses Algie had so often seen on the beach. Her sightless eyes stared up at the stars. A puddle of dark liquid stained the flagstones around her.

Drawn by Algie's silence, Frankie and Lulu shouldered past. Lulu dropped to her knees and put two fingers against Madam's throat, while Frankie crouched by her head. Even in his horror, Algie wondered at the number of odd skills the sisters possessed.

"She's breathing," Frankie said, and slapped Madam's face.

"Frankie!" Algie exclaimed. Frankie slapped Madam again, and then shook her shoulders.

"Out cold," she said. "Go get—" Her voice trailed off.

"Algie," Lulu whispered. "Come look."

Feeling numb and disembodied, Algie stepped out the window and tiptoed through the dark puddle. Colors and outlines seemed sharp and unreal, like the time his doctor changed his medication and he'd lain in bed for a day while dream-monsters stalked the ceiling. This nightmare was real, though. And a growing dread in his stomach told him it was about to get worse.

Frankie pulled aside the ruffles of Madam's collar.

Livid, ring-shaped bruises disfigured Madam's throat. The sleeves of her dress were torn, and similar bruises marked her arms.

Sucker bruises.

The liquid that Lulu knelt in was not blood. It was ink.

CHAPTER

30

"**WHAT ARE YOU** doing here?" the doctor said, as he tripped over Algie outside Madam's room.

"Is Madam awake?" Algie asked.

"Still comatose, and she doesn't need a bunch of children hanging around. Clear out."

Algie, Frankie, and Lulu cleared out, but only around the corner. There they reconvened their meeting.

"Maybe she's faking it," Lulu said.

Frankie shook her head. "I stuck a pin all the way into her arm before they carried her off. She would have flinched if she were faking. Don't worry, no one saw," she added, in response to Algie's shocked look.

"You already slapped her. Wasn't that enough?"

"Probably." Frankie grinned. "It can't hurt to make sure. Besides, how could I pass up the chance? You heard how she yelled at me that time I borrowed her trapeze."

"Did you ever think there might be a reason she's grumpy all the time?"

"Like what?"

"I don't know," Algie said. "Maybe she doesn't feel well. Or maybe she's frightened or worried about something."

"That's no excuse. If she has reasons, she should get over them."

"She might be trying," Algie said. "And I don't think it's very nice to stick pins into unconscious people."

"'Nice.'" Frankie sneered. "You think that's so important?"

"I do." Algie could not verbalize how he felt. Possibly due to his own recent failures in that regard, he was starting to realize how important it was to treat everyone with patience and respect, no matter his personal feelings toward them. But even if he found the words, Frankie might only laugh. She always got aggressive when she felt scared or angry.

"When I was upset with Everett," Algie said, "I got carried away and said things that weren't nice. It caused a big problem, and we both stopped listening to each other. Maybe if . . ." A shiver shook his stomach as he trailed off. Everett had tried to warn him that something like this might happen.

"Madam Maximus isn't our family," Frankie said. "And she isn't a nice person, so I didn't care. She probably did something awful to make Octavia attack her."

171

"But we don't know for certain that Octavia did attack her," Lulu said. "Maybe it was Angel. She can't stand Madam."

Frankie shook her head. "If Angel wanted to bump someone off, she'd do it. Madam's alive, so it wasn't Angel. Besides, how do you explain those bruises? And the ink?"

"Maybe Angel is trying to frame Octavia?"

"The bruises could have been caused by something else," Algie suggested. "A chain?" He couldn't stand the thought of their gentle friend committing such violence. But the paralyzed boar he had met in the swamp haunted him. If Octavia thought Madam was after her babies . . . a vision of Jasper's lifeless body swung across his mind, followed by Everett's voice. *If you kids aren't careful, someone's going to get hurt.*

"What if—" He swallowed, forcing the words. "What if this is our fault?"

CHAPTER

31

"A FIFTY-FOOT giant octopus?"

"Pounced on Madam during her after-dinner walk. She told the doctor when she woke up this morning. Would have dragged her off to its lair if the prof's cat and those kids hadn't scared it away."

"Mr. Davenport left for New York this morning. Said he'll bring back a passel of big-game hunters to exterminate it."

"We can take care of the situation before the big boys get here. Think what a trophy it would make!"

Algie, Lulu, and Frankie exchanged miserable glances. They picked up their breakfast trays and moved farther away from the table of the enthusiastic, muscular gentlemen. But their new neighbors were no better.

"Such a turn it gave me to see her lying there." Lady Plumworthy wafted an egret-feather fan. "I fainted, of course. It will probably send me into a decline."

"You didn't have hysterics like I did," said Mrs. Emsworth, sitting up straighter. "When I saw my dear boy covered in ink—to think it might have been *him* lying there!"

"I feel light-headed remembering it," chimed a third lady. "In fact—oh dear, I'm going to swoon—"

"I wish people would stop talking about Octavia." Lulu covered her face with her hands. "Then maybe I could stop thinking about it."

"There's no use pretending it didn't happen," Frankie said. "Madam Maximus saw Octavia attack."

"We don't know that," Algie insisted. "The story might have gotten blown out of proportion." His fear from the night before could not be true. He would not believe it.

Angel O'Dare sauntered over to their table.

"You're the ones who discovered Madam?" She picked at a hangnail.

"Yes," Algie said warily. The sharp glance Angel had darted at him contradicted her casual attitude.

"Were you scared?" Angel asked. "What—what did it feel like?"

"Ask them." Frankie waved her hand at the neighboring ladies. "If you're doing research on fear, they'll describe every chill until they faint from lack of oxygen."

"Will they?" Angel looked up from her fingernail. "Excuse me."

"What was that about?" Lulu crinkled her eyebrows as Angel moved off toward the circle of ladies.

"Forget her," Frankie said. "Listen, you two—we won't be able to figure out why Octavia attacked until we know what happened."

"But how can we find out?" Lulu asked. "They won't let us talk to Madam."

Frankie patted her rope. "That's where this comes in."

★

Algie wrapped his sweaty hands around the top of the window arch, wedged his foot between two decorative bricks, and hauled himself higher. Wind tugged at his shirt and blew dust into his eyes. The roiling clouds seemed too close. He would have fallen long ago if not for the steady tension Frankie and Lulu were applying on the rope stretched taut above his head.

"Put more weight on your feet," Lulu called. Both she and Frankie stood in the fifth-floor gutter, lashed to a merman statue. Frankie was belaying Algie off a carabiner attached to their anchor ropes.

"Easy for you to say," Algie gasped. Half-clinging, half-lying on the window arch, he let go with his right hand and slapped for the gutter. His hand missed, and he peeled off the ledge into space.

Algie sucked in his breath as the lawn flashed below. Twirling, he swung back and smacked into the wall. Crushed-shell concrete scraped his elbows.

"Grab anything," Frankie grunted. "We'll pull you the rest of the way if you help."

Algie regained the window ledge and tried again. This time, he made it to the gutter. He rolled onto his back, closing his eyes to shut out the clouds.

"Remind me," he panted, "never to believe either of you when you say 'trust us, it'll be easy.'"

Frankie snorted at his imitation of her drawl. "Everything's easy when it's over." She reached down and unclipped Algie's rope.

"Hey!" Algie flattened himself in the gutter.

"Madam's balcony is right there," Lulu said. "It's like walking on a sidewalk."

"You mean it'll be easy?"

"Of course—" Lulu caught herself and laughed. "Maybe you should stay clipped in until you're over the railing."

Algie tried to smile, but his face felt strained. Soon they would know the truth.

They climbed onto Madam Maximus's balcony, and Algie knocked on the glass door.

The curtains yanked back, and Angel appeared with startling abruptness. Before she could say anything, Lulu jerked the door open and wriggled beneath her elbow.

"Please, Madam Maximus," she said. "We wanted to talk to you, and they wouldn't let us in. I promise we won't stay long."

Algie pulled the bouquet from his knapsack. It looked crumpled after their climb, but the crushed flowers smelled nice. Angel's shoulders blocked his view of the room.

"May I give her this?" he asked.

"Let them in," called Madam's weak voice.

Angel stepped aside to let Algie and Frankie pass, then walked into the adjoining sitting room. Before she shut the door, her gray eyes lingered on Madam's prostrate form in the bed. It was not a look of sympathy.

As the door clicked shut behind Angel, Madam wriggled higher on her pillows and took Algie's bouquet of flowers. Her normally florid face was pale, bruises showing purple beneath the collar of her bathrobe.

"So sweet of you to think of me. I love gardenias."

"Madam," Frankie said, "will you please tell us what happened last night?"

"It's a strange story, isn't it? I suppose it's natural you children should be curious. I'm sorry they wouldn't let you in. There's nothing like a child to make one feel better."

Algie reflected that Madam Maximus's views on children seemed to have changed since the day Frankie "borrowed" her circus equipment. Madam had made several strong remarks on the subject while chasing Frankie with her ringmistress's whip. Still, it seemed reasonable that a brush with death might change one's perspective.

"I was strolling the covered walkway," Madam began, "as usual after dinner—doing three laps round the building does wonders for the digestion—when I became aware of a pair of yellow eyes watching me from the coconut grove. Naturally, I was curious."

"Naturally," Frankie said.

"I walked toward them—and the Beast wriggled out of the shadows."

"What did it look like?" Algie tried not to wriggle himself.

"What did it look like? You mean, what *was* it. I saw it clearly in the moonlight. It was an octopus—like that pet of yours that unlocked my writing desk, young man. Only this one was immense . . . immense, but beautiful." A misty expression passed over Madam's face. Then she shuddered. "It writhed right up to me. Of course, I was terrified. I started to run. It came after me and caught me around the waist. I fell to the ground and screamed. The scream must have frightened it. I felt a sharp pain and tentacles wrapping around my neck—"

"Arms," Frankie said.

"I said neck." Madam Maximus looked miffed.

"Octopuses have arms," Frankie said. "Arms have suckers all the way up. Tentacles only have suckers near the end."

Judging by Madam's expression, she was reconsidering her reformed views on children—at least where Frankie was concerned. Algie stepped on Frankie's foot.

"Thank you," he said. "We're sorry for having disturbed you. I hope you feel better."

"Wait," Madam called as they turned to leave. "Do you know if the beast is still at large?"

Algie swallowed. "Mr. Davenport is bringing in a team of hunters."

Madam nodded. Her face was sad.

"I suppose it's for the best," she said. "But it's a terrible pity. You'll think I'm ridiculous, but . . . I have the strangest feeling the creature didn't mean to hurt me. You'd almost think it was playing."

CHAPTER

32

"**IT WAS OUR** fault all along," Frankie said into her hands. They were in the lakeside boathouse, in the laboratory of the *Diving Belle*. It was the only place they could escape hearing about the attack. "If we hadn't gotten Octavia used to people, she wouldn't have gone galloping up to Madam. She never did before."

The rising wind shook the doors to the boathouse.

"What should we have done?" Lulu's eyes were pink with suppressed tears. "Walked away and never seen them again?"

"I don't know." Algie rubbed his aching temples. "I thought it was so important that we study them. Scientific knowledge is important. I didn't think—"

"None of us thought," Frankie said. "Not enough. We didn't want to. We were too busy daydreaming about the publicity splash we were going to make. We didn't care about what might be best for the octopuses. Or the guests. Or anyone but ourselves."

"How do you balance it?" Algie asked. "Science, people, and nature—how do you give everything its due?"

No one answered.

After a moment, Frankie lifted her head. She had a red splotch across her forehead where it had rested on the table, but her eyes held what Algie dubbed her "Joan of Arc" look—the one that said she would carry her goal if she had to take over an army to do it.

"We're not going to have another Jasper situation," she said. "Here's what we'll do."

★

Algie squinted out the *Diving Belle*'s cabin at the gusts of wind driving choppy waves across the water. The Señora's Spring was not blue anymore, but iron-gray.

"Are you sure we shouldn't wait till tomorrow?" he asked.

"This day was made for us." Frankie had her feet apart, hands on the wheel. "If the weather were nice, the beach and swamp would be clogged with octopus hunters. It's now or never."

Algie glanced at Lulu, but she shook her head.

"Frankie's right," she said. "Are you still worrying about your family, Algie?"

"Mother will have a fit when she finds my note."

"By that time, we'll be halfway to Cuba—and so will the octopuses." Frankie gripped the helm tighter. "Don't lose your nerve, able seaman. This is a matter of life or death. We got the octopuses into this mess, and no grownup is going to help us get them out."

"Do you really think the red tide won't reach to Cuba?" Algie asked.

"We'll check the beaches for dead animals. Besides, we've got the microscope in the lab. We'll pick out a nice, healthy, deserted lagoon, and everyone can be happy."

Algie nodded. He knew the octopi needed relocating. But his stomach felt as choppy as the surface of the headspring.

They moored the *Belle* on the far side of the spring, then loaded the pirogue with an old pickle barrel. The trees sheltered them from the wind as they poled through the swamp. Since the octopi were most comfortable around Algie, the children agreed he should be the one to package them. He tied a rope around his waist.

"Don't hesitate if Octavia gets aggressive," Lulu said. "Yank the line and we'll pull you out."

The morning was so overcast that Algie could see nothing as they lowered him into the cave. He switched on the waterproof flashlight Frankie had given him. Its beam glittered off the wet limestone and flashed across Octavia's bulk peering from her nest of junk.

"Just me," Algie said. He shivered as the water slid up around his neck. That submerged crevice below . . . no, he would not think about it. The pickle barrel splashed softly as it landed beside him. Holding the flashlight in one hand and pushing the barrel with the other, Algie dogpaddled to the ledge. To his relief, all eight babies were there.

"We're going on an adventure." Algie patted each octopus as he filled the barrel with water and placed them inside. He looked around for Octavia and jumped to discover her right behind him. Her sensitive suckers explored the barrel, but she did not seem tense. Her yellow eyes were trusting.

Algie tugged on the ropes, one for him and one for the barrel. "Ready," he called.

Foot by foot, the girls hauled Algie and the octopi up. As soon as he could, Algie grabbed the lip of the opening and crawled out. Dirt and dead leaves stuck to his clothes, but he brushed them off and turned around. The next few minutes would tell if the rest of the evacuation would be easy, or very difficult indeed.

The children held their breath, waiting. Then a rubbery arm poked out of the cave, followed by another.

Algie's muscles relaxed. Octavia was following. Sucker by sucker, her massive body oozed from the hole.

They kept to the deepest waterways as they headed back to the *Belle*. Octavia remained a patient shadow, her eyes fixed on the barrel of babies. Though it was still windy, the sun came out as they reached the headspring.

"We need to get out of here." Lulu glanced shoreward as they hoisted the barrel of octopi aboard the *Belle*. "Sunshine means people, and people mean trouble . . . Octavia, *please* stay underwater until we're out to sea."

Frankie scurried around the barge, doing last-minute checks of everything from charts to lifebelts to provisions.

"Canned goods . . . emergency flare pistols . . . we have all eight babies?" she said to Algie. "Did you double-check? Did you triple?"

"I know how to count." Algie frowned. "Look yourself if it'll make you feel better. But don't blame me if they come pouring out all over the place."

Frankie unlatched the barrel lid and leaned over the opening. She counted, frowned, and counted again.

"I see Monday through Sunday," she said. "Where's Pulpy?"

"Let me look." Algie counted. He counted again.

"It's my fault for not double-checking while we were at the cave." Frankie scrunched her hands in her hair. "I should have done the whole thing myself."

"A pack of ladies came out on the lawn," Lulu reported. "We've got to get out of here. Octavia, stay down!"

Octavia's massive arm crawled over the railing as she felt for the cabin door. Frankie and Algie ran to soothe her, and to block the sight from the hotel with their bodies. At last they coaxed her back underwater.

"You girls take the boat down to the pier." Algie's nerves were zinging, stung by the fresh proof of his own incompetence. "I'll go back and get Pulpy."

"You stay here," Frankie said. "We don't need you wasting any more time."

"It's my mistake and I'm going to fix it," Algie snapped. "Besides, Pulpy likes me better. We don't need *you* crawling around in the dark trying to find him, and we can't leave Lulu alone with Octavia."

"Be quiet, both of you." Lulu guided the barge along the bank, heading for the main river. "Let him go, Frankie—he's right about Pulpy. We'll wait for him at the ocean dock."

But Algie's bravado oozed away as he found himself punting alone through the swamp. What if Pulpy decided to hide? Would Frankie and Lulu leave him behind? Or maybe he would delay the whole mission and they'd be discovered. Octavia would become a trophy on the wall of the professor's mysterious collector—or, worse, a prisoner in a tank. And it would all be Algie's fault. He had counted the babies before he put on the lid. But they were so squirmy, and Pulpy was so wily . . .

A clump of treetops rustled. Algie looked up, and his pirogue rammed the bank. Shaken, he got out and moored the boat to a waterside branch. It was time to hike to the cave anyway.

But as he tromped through the undergrowth, Algie could not shake the sensation of watching eyes. He remembered what Frankie had said yesterday, about imagining Angel creeping through the trees.

"Who's there?" he called.

A crow flapped past, squawking. Then the leaves of a strangler fig shook right above him. As the rustling grew louder, Algie's heart began to pound. He licked dry lips and picked up a stick.

The leaves parted. A pink-faced monkey peered curiously at Algie.

Algie laughed in relief. It was one of the escaped macaques Lulu had told him about.

"Don't worry," he said to the monkey. "I won't bother you."

The macaque screamed and bounced off through the trees.

"I don't think it's worried," said a voice above him. "But you should be."

CHAPTER

33

MADAM MAXIMUS DROPPED from a branch. But not the pale, languishing Madam who Algie had visited that morning. She was fully dressed, with her whip and sequined ringmistress's coat. Even the bruises had vanished from her neck. Algie was too shocked to be frightened.

"How did you—aren't you supposed to be in bed?"

Madam laughed. "My 'attack' was beautifully staged, wasn't it? A little theatrical makeup does wonders."

"Staged? You mean Octavia never—" Relief flooded Algie's heart. Their friend had not hurt anyone! Then anger overtook him. "Why would you do that? Now every hunter in the state will be after her."

"Because I needed your help to capture her family. Do you have any idea what even one of those creatures is worth? I do. I telegraphed the professor's collector yesterday."

"How did you know about that?"

"None of your business. I suspected something—*fishy*, if you will—was going on ever since she got hold of my ankle in the spring. But I didn't realize the full possibilities until I spotted her with you in the greenhouse yesterday. A tame monster and her tame little handler!"

"Octavia and the babies never did anything to you," Algie said. "Why would you want to hurt them?"

"Who said I wanted to hurt them? All I want to do is to sell them."

"But why?" Algie persisted. "What more do you need? You have a successful circus. You can afford to spend the winter here!" He waved an arm at the moss-draped branches, the shimmering dragonflies and palm fronds.

Madam Maximus's eyes narrowed in scorn.

"Spoken like a young person. Someday you'll learn things aren't always what they seem. How would you feel lying awake every night, knowing each day might be your last?" She turned away, but not before Algie had glimpsed the same fear and misery that he had seen in her eyes once already. His anger softened.

"Is that how you feel?" he asked.

"I was diagnosed with a heart complaint over a year ago." Madam rubbed her hands to hide their trembling. "I've spent every available penny and more on treatments and consultations.

No one suspects yet, but the circus is financially ruined. If I can't find a cure, I could die at any moment." She sniffed and brushed her eyes.

Algie offered his handkerchief.

"My only chance," Madam continued, ignoring it, "is an experimental medicine, but it costs a fortune. When I saw that glorious invertebrate gold mine you call Octavia . . . well, I knew she was my salvation."

"Did you tell your acrobats about your heart problem?" Algie asked.

Madam laughed again—a harsh, unhappy sound. "You can't show weakness to the pack. Fortunately, the cash incentive was enough to overcome their scruples about octopus poaching. There'll be enough for the medicine and plenty left over."

"I think you should tell them," Algie said. "And I'm sorry, but I'm not going to help you capture the octopi."

"My dear, you already have. You packaged them up and delivered them to my doorstep." Madam checked her wristwatch. "Your friends should have reached the ocean dock by now, so the troupe will have neutralized them."

"Frankie and Lulu will never let you take them." Algie tried hard to keep fear from his voice.

"They won't have a choice. I 'borrowed' the professor's tranquilizer gun—in fact, I used it on myself last night to simulate the octopus's toxic nip. That notebook of yours was invaluable. It's a pity you'll never become a naturalist."

Algie grabbed his knapsack and began to run.

189

Leaves shook. He looked up. Madam Maximus was swinging through the trees beside him, swooping from branch to branch. He had to get away from the trees—but there *was* no getting away from trees here.

Hoping to lose her in the undergrowth, Algie dug in his heels and doubled back. Above him, Madam leaped and caught a vine. Algie ran faster, clawing his way through leaves.

Her huge ruffled form slammed into him. Algie was knocked off his feet and carried away. Madam Maximus held him under her arm, sailing through the air on the vine like it was one of Angel's aerial silks. Her hat feathers fluttered as they swung upward.

"Let me go!" Algie yelled, as fiercely as he could with his head clamped between Madam's bicep and ribs. He tried to kick her shins but encountered layers of skirt.

"Certainly," Madam said, and released him at the apex of the swing.

Algie seemed to float level with the treetops. Then his stomach turned a flip, and he dropped. Past the leaves, past the tree trunks, through a palmetto clump—

SPLOOSH.

Disoriented, Algie paddled at the water. Bubbles streamed sideways past his face. He swam as hard as he could after them. His head broke the surface. Moist, earthy air filled his lungs.

Shaking the water out of his eyes, Algie squinted up at a blurry circle of light that was the opening to the octopi's cavern. A feathery-hatted head leaned over and waved.

"So you don't feel too alone while you're waiting to die,"

Madam said, "know that your friends will be jettisoned over-board halfway between here and Pensacola. It's unfortunate, but I can't leave any witnesses. I'm sure you understand. When your mother finds your note, everyone will assume you all three were a casualty of the very sea monster you tried to save."

"Don't you dare hurt them!" Algie shouted, but his words came out a gurgle. Foliage cracked and rustled, then leafy branches covered the hole.

"Not that anyone will find you out here." Madam's voice filtered through the leaves. "Goodbye, Algie."

Her footsteps receded into silence. Bubbles from his plunge simmered up around Algie, fizzing as they joined the air. Even if someone eventually found him, it would be too late for Frankie and Lulu.

If he were stronger, he could rock-climb up the wall and across the ceiling to save his friends. If only it were Frankie stuck here, or even Everett. Algie had never felt so inadequate. The current from the crack at the bottom of the spring swept past his legs. Frankie had once told him that most of the springs in the area were connected through an underwater cave network. If only he had gills, he could escape through the passageways. But if-only's would not help him now.

Octavia's nest glimmered in the blue gloom. The statue of the mother stood tranquil and silent. Algie turned his face away so she would not see his despair. But he felt her eyes on the back of his head. Taking a breath, he dove toward the only place she could not look at him—into the nest itself.

It was dark inside when Algie surfaced, but a sliver of light shone through a crack in the roof and pierced the water. Algie climbed onto the wedged rowboat, pulled his knees to his chest, and dropped his forehead onto them.

His knapsack wriggled.

"Pulpy!" Algie shook him out and hugged him. "You should have gone with the girls! Or maybe you shouldn't have," he added, his elation streaming away.

Pulpy wrapped his arms around Algie's wrist and squiggled. He did not know his family was about to become expensive trophies.

Algie groaned. "I failed, Pulpy." He swallowed, unable to continue. Saying it aloud was too terrible. He hugged the little animal to his cheek. "I'm sorry."

Pulpy slithered free and shambled to the rowboat's edge. Algie watched as he examined a broken bottle, tossed it away, and scooted toward the next shiny object. Something glinted in the thin stream of light, lodged in the wall of the nest.

Algie pried it free. It was a metal helmet. Dozens of circular viewing ports studded the faceplate.

"The Señora's diving helmet," Algie whispered.

CHAPTER

34

ALGIE COULDN'T BELIEVE IT. The same helmet he'd seen sketched in the library notebook. In what lonely crack had Octavia discovered it, bringing it back to decorate her home?

The idea of the submerged-cave network shimmered across Algie's mind. He might not have gills . . . but now he might not need them.

His body crackling with energy, Algie plunged into the water. Holding his breath, he swam to the bottom of the nest and floated upward, scanning every inch of the sides. Then he swam outside and crawled on top, searching through the high-piled junk. There! A metal boot, hidden beneath a branch.

The body of the suit was jammed deep in the nest. Standing in the stern of the wedged rowboat, Algie pulled and tugged.

When he finally dragged the suit free, the nest's whole structure collapsed. The statue of the mother and baby slipped to the bottom of the pool and landed upright beneath the skylight.

The rowboat floated free, carrying Algie and the heavy suit. Algie emptied it of water as best he could, then climbed inside. A mildew-y smell and the sharp tang of metal filled his nose. Fuzzy dark-green algae squished against his arms.

Algie peered over the side of the boat. Below him, among the bones, the dark crevice waited. How far to the bottom? And how much farther did that crack go on? Algie's heart flip-flopped. But he screwed on the helmet.

The image of the Señora gulping for oxygen in some underwater labyrinth, slipping out of the suit and swimming frantically for light and air, flashed before his eyes. The breathless desperation was too familiar. He twisted the helmet off in a panic.

"Stop," he said aloud to his imagination. The Señora had perished in the quest of knowledge, doing what she loved. She knew the risks before she began and decided they were worth it. Algie screwed on the helmet again and took a breath. So far, so good. The smothering had been in his mind.

The diving suit's joints were stiff but watertight. Peering through the eye-windows, Algie wrapped his metal fingers around his knapsack and took out the flashlight. He didn't know how much air the suit held, but he didn't have time to test it. Every minute brought Frankie and Lulu closer to doom.

Pulpy zoomed back and forth through the water beside the rowboat. Algie heaved several fast, deep breaths, switched on the flashlight, and dove. His heart floated into his throat as he sank. The same claustrophobic fear he'd felt in the diving bell gripped him.

His feet struck bottom. Waterweed fluttered and waved around Algie's knees in the garden of rocks and bones. Tiny bubbles glimmered beneath the beam of his flashlight as Pulpy jetted circles around his head.

Step by ponderous step, Algie made for the great crevice at the bottom of the spring. When he came to the edge, he stopped. Could he do it, even for the girls? Surely one of the would-be octopus hunters would find him before he starved. But both Davenports would be dead by then, the octopi lost forever. He had to take the chance that the spring had other outlets.

"You don't have to feel brave," Algie whispered to himself. His voice echoed inside the helmet. "You just have to do it." He shut his eyes, lifted his foot, and jumped.

It was like falling down the rabbit hole in *Alice's Adventures in Wonderland.* Algie half-expected to see an empty jar of orange marmalade slide past on one of the rocks.

Thump. The landing pulsed through his body.

He stood in a limestone cavern. Shining his light in all directions, Algie saw nothing but honeycombing tunnels. He picked a passage at random and began to walk. The effort of moving the stiff, clumsy suit soon became agony. Was it sweat dripping down his chest, or had the suit sprung a leak? His breath fogged the eyeholes, and he could not wipe them; instead, he held his breath until they cleared. The inside of the suit was hot and stifling. Algie began to wheeze. He could not tell if the tightness in his chest was asthma or lack of oxygen.

How long had he been walking? If it hadn't been for Pulpy's exuberant presence, despair would have overwhelmed him long ago. A sandy-colored eel slipped past his feet, but no other living thing disturbed them. No algae, no fish, no crustaceans—even the floors were bare rock and sand. Algie began to feel as though he were wandering through a deserted beehive.

Once again the tunnel branched. Chest heaving, Algie lifted his hand to wipe the sweat off his forehead and encountered the bulky helmet. Right or left? More lives than one depended on his choice. He shone his flashlight down one tunnel, then the other, searching for a clue.

The flashlight went out.

Blackness. Despair. Death.

And then . . . Algie caught his breath in a choking gasp. A sparkling galaxy had blazed into being, zipping back and forth past his face. It was Pulpy, shining with bioluminescence, a chorus of lights in the endless dark. Blindly, holding his hands out in front of him, Algie followed.

His hands hit rock. Algie looked up and spotted Pulpy, dancing invitingly overhead. The rock was not a sheer wall like Algie had first thought, but slanted like a tilted chimney. Bracing a foot and arm on each side of the tunnel, Algie began to climb.

Was it his imagination, or could he see dim shapes? It was growing lighter! Algie squeezed around a bend, and the angle flattened to a slope. Ahead shone a pale circle. The mouth of the tunnel lay before him.

Algie staggered forward—and stopped. The edges of his suit ground against stone.

Algie turned sideways and tried to edge past, but the bulbous joints and shoulders of the suit would not fit. To make matters worse, he was pretty sure his breathlessness was no longer due to asthma. He had to act, and quickly.

Pulpy hovered at the tunnel's exit. Algie took a step backward, inflated his lungs, and unscrewed his helmet.

Water poured into the suit before he could get the helmet off. Fear almost snatched his breath, but Algie forced his shaking muscles to keep going. He threw the helmet aside and wriggled out of the suit, then swam as hard as he could after Pulpy. The pale circle widened and became sky. He was at the bottom of the headspring.

Algie swam as he had never swum before. His arms and legs lost feeling, but he kicked and paddled ceaselessly, his entire being bent on that rippling ceiling. Schools of startled fish darted past. His ribs began to heave.

Algie clenched his throat, feeling like he was going to throw up. His body was taking over. Any second it would breathe and flood his lungs. His vision began to blur, and he shut his eyes. He was not doing this for himself alone. It was for Frankie—Mother—Lulu—Everett. It was for his past self, afraid he was incapable of anything important.

His head burst out into wind and chop. Algie gasped huge lungfuls of air while Pulpy cavorted and jetted beside him. After catching his breath, he struck out in long strokes, heading for shore and the hotel.

CHAPTER

35

ALGIE FOUND EVERETT in the coffee shop, his face buried in his arms. Empty mugs of hot chocolate scattered the table.

"They're gone." Everett rolled his head side to side. "The whole troupe. Angel O'Dare, the only girl I've ever loved . . ."

Algie remained unmoved. If his brother was in love with the star of an octopus-poaching circus act, he needed to be disillusioned.

Everett turned his head and saw Algie, scratched, damp, and dirty. "What do you want?"

"I need help," Algie said.

"That makes sense. I can't think of any other reason you'd be talking to me."

"I can," Algie said, ticking them off on his fingers. "You're my brother, I miss you, and I wish I'd listened when you tried to talk to me before."

"You're saying that because you want something."

"No," Algie said. "I'm saying it because even when we disagree, I care about your opinion." His time in the cave had taught him that never again did he want to stand on pride with family. It didn't matter who reached out first.

Everett eyed him. Algie held his gaze steady, heart thumping behind his collarbone. He wouldn't get far without Everett.

Wilting, Everett rolled his face back into his forearms.

"I haven't been a very good brother this trip." His sleeves muffled his voice. "Believe me, I know that better than you do."

"Neither of us has." Algie slid into the chair beside him.

"But I'm older. And I *do* try. But every time I bungle things, I get angry at myself, and that makes me angry at *you*; and you're such a pepperpot, it sets me off—"

Algie coughed. "We can forget all that."

"And now the troupe is gone . . . Angel O'Dare, the only girl I've ever loved . . . "

"I know," said Algie, seizing his opportunity. "I was just down at the pier. They've taken their three-masted ship. We need to telegraph the Coast Guard."

"Do you think they're in trouble?" Everett sat up and looked out the window. The weather had worsened. Wind lashed the palm trees and huffed against the glass.

"Telegraph wires are down," said the shopkeeper. "It might be weeks before they're repaired." He set down another mug of hot chocolate. Everett passed it to Algie.

"You look like you need it. What happened to you?"

As quickly as he could, Algie explained. The shopkeeper listened with interest.

"That's a good story," he said when Algie finished.

"It's not a story," Algie said. "If we can't reach the Coast Guard, we'll need a fleet of the fastest yachts to catch up with Madam."

Everett cast him a look that was half-impressed, half-quizzical. Algie flushed but held his gaze. To Everett, he had always been the sick younger brother, weak and idealistic. If Everett were to follow him now, Algie needed to command his respect as well as love.

"You couldn't catch her even if you found someone who'd risk their boat in this storm," the shopkeeper said. "It looks bad now, but it's about to get worse." He poured himself a mug of chocolate and downed it with one swig. "Take it from me, young man—whatever yarn those two Davenport rascals spun you, don't believe it. They love a ruckus more than a lizard loves sunshine. Ten to one they're off with their dad in New York."

"It *does* sound far-fetched." Everett chewed his lip.

"You don't believe me?" For a minute, Algie felt worse than he had in the cave.

"Oh, I believe you," Everett said. "But we'll have a hard time convincing anyone else. So this octopus thing is a friend of yours? The one that attacked Madam Maximus?"

"That was a hoax." Algie hopped with joy, he was so thankful for Everett's vote of confidence. "Madam knew we'd try to rescue the octopi, and we played straight into her hands."

"You have a photograph?"

"Madam Maximus stole it. I do have this." Algie pulled Pulpy from his knapsack and plunked him down on the table. Everett's eyes sparked with adventure, then dimmed.

"Yachts won't do us any good," he said. "Like this fellow says, we'd never catch up." The shopkeeper nodded in agreement, running hot water over his mugs.

Algie stared at the clock on the wall. Gears whirred in his mind.

"Maybe a yacht won't do the trick," he said. "But I know something that might."

★

After Algie whispered his plan, he and Everett stood up.

One table over, a man lowered the newspaper covering his face. It was Parker James, Everett's rival for Angel's attention.

"Excuse me," Parker said, "but I couldn't help overhearing. I think I know someone who can help you."

"Who?" Algie asked.

"A well-known author who's wintering here," Parker said. "Recovering from a bad case of writer's block."

Everett asked, "But how could they help?"

For his answer, Parker rose and led the way out of the café. Algie and Everett followed, exchanging looks.

They rounded a corner, and the windswept lawn appeared. The professor's airship loomed beside the boathouse, its great canopy rippling in the gale. It was battened down with multiple ropes and anchors, bobbing on the water as it sheltered from the storm.

Parker was not looking at the airship. His gaze was directed through the nearest French window. Inside a cozy study, surrounded by high-backed armchairs and a crackling fire, Angel O'Dare was playing a solitary game of pool.

Parker nodded toward her.

"There she is," he said to the brothers. "Good luck." He strolled off.

"You're a well-known author?" Algie asked, scrambling through the window.

"To my constant regret." Angel sunk the seven-ball with a clack and chalked her cue. "I wish I'd never written that *Haleyford* book. But I was so bored, I had to do *something*! Who knew a second one would be this hard to write? I've been sneaking around every spooky location I can find, trying to scare up some inspiration."

"You're Godric Featheringstone III?" Algie gaped. "So that's why you were in the greenhouse the night you saw Octavia!"

Everett spluttered. "I thought you left with Madam Maximus!"

Angel cracked her back, pulling the pool cue behind her shoulders. "Madam gave me a two-week vacation for helping her with a promotional stunt."

"Did you do her makeup for the attack?" Algie asked.

Angel's right eyebrow flickered. "How did you guess? Madam will murder me if she thinks I blabbed."

"I believe it," Algie said. "She tried to murder me too. Listen, we have a problem, and Parker said you would help."

"Did he?" This time, both Angel's eyebrows went up. "I'm listening."

By the time Algie finished, Angel looked more interested than he had ever seen her.

"I've been trying to get fired all winter," she said, "and Madam won't let me off my contract. But I think even she might let me go if I pirate her ship and swipe her tame monster. Plus Parker's right—it'll make great copy for my next book."

"Wait," Everett said. "Why'd you tell Parker about the book and not me?"

Angel flexed her fingers and shook out her arms, then turned a back walkover.

"When do we start?" she asked, coming right-side up.

"As soon as Professor Champion agrees to lend his airship," Algie said.

"Which won't be happening," said a voice from one of the high-backed chairs.

Everyone whirled.

Professor Champion rose from the chair, his hands full of fishing tackle.

"Don't look so surprised," he said. "As a top-notch naturalist, I can blend with my surroundings when necessary."

"Professor!" Everett said. "We need your airship to rescue the Davenports!"

"No," said Professor Champion.

"If Madam said she'd toss those kids in the drink," said Angel, "she will, believe me."

"An understandable impulse. I don't know if you've noticed, but neither of those juveniles have endeared themselves to me. Ordinarily I would agree to recover them in exchange for the octopuses, but in this case I wash my hands of it." The professor's smile twisted. "Professor Ransom Champion is too wise a man to step between Augusta Maximus and her plans."

"You told me you were worried about their safety!" Everett yelped. "Were you stringing me along the whole time?"

"I had to enlist your help somehow, didn't I? Although you proved useless in the end. All that time, and you couldn't wring a single drop of information from your brother." Professor Champion shook his head. "Families these days."

Angel stepped forward. Her pool cue flashed in the firelight as she flipped it through the air and caught it.

"If you won't lend us the airship," she said, "we'll have to commandeer it."

Faster than Algie's eye could follow, Professor Champion's

elbow flicked. A whir, a flash of silver, and Angel yelled. Her pool cue thudded to the carpet.

Algie's stomach turned sick. A barbed fishhook dangled from Angel's eyelid.

"At the moment, the hook is superficially embedded in the subcutaneous tissue of the right inner canthus," said the professor. "My dear, I wouldn't do that," he said as Angel raised her hand. Holding on to the other end of the line, the professor rose and strolled across the room. Angel followed jerkily.

"At the moment, the hook can be removed with minimal difficulty," Professor Champion resumed. "But one twitch of my hand and the barb will embed in the cornea. The young lady may lose her vision, or possibly the entire eye. Not an ideal situation for a tightrope artist."

No one moved.

"Miss O'Dare and I will stroll down to the *Flying Dancer*," Professor Champion said. "I will release her and sail on my merry way. The three of you will leave me in peace and—"

Smash. A leaded crystal vase descended on the professor's head.

Professor Champion swayed. His eyes crossed, and he toppled to the carpet. Behind him stood Mrs. Emsworth.

"Let me look at that eyelid, dear," she said to Angel. Her voice shook, but her hands were steady as they set down the vase. "I trained as a nurse with the National Aid Society during the Siege of Paris, you know."

CHAPTER

36

TO ALGIE'S SURPRISE, his mother did not faint at the sight of Angel's wound. She insisted on cleaning it with iodine, then turned her attention to Professor Champion.

"My blood fairly boiled when I heard him refuse to help," Mrs. Emsworth said. "Not too tight, dear," she said to Angel; "we don't want to cut off his circulation."

With a look that said she was going against her own wishes, Angel loosened the cords around Professor Champion's wrists and ankles. The professor could only glare, since his mouth was obscured by Mrs. Emsworth's best lavender-scented handkerchief. Angel took his legs, Mrs. Emsworth his wrists, and they stashed him behind a sofa.

"And now," said Mrs. Emsworth, dusting her hands, "we have an airship to commandeer. Algie, once those poor Davenport girls are safe, you and I are going to have a chat about what you've been doing this whole time. Not bathing quietly in the mineral springs, I'm beginning to suspect."

Algie and Everett exchanged secret, awed glances. Was it yesterday that Algie had doubted whether his mother would jump on an alligator for him? Any alligator had better watch out.

When all necessary equipment had been gathered, the boarding party fought through the wind toward the boathouse. Topiary animals tugged and strained at their roots, and fallen palm branches littered the lawn.

"Mother," Everett called over the gale. "Why didn't you ever tell us you'd been through a war?"

"There are a good many things I haven't told you, Everett." Mrs. Emsworth spoke through a mouthful of hatpins as she secured her hat. "And this is no time to chat about family history. You won't find that airship unguarded, unless I'm much mistaken."

She was right. Two figures paced the *Dancer*'s deck.

"Only two?" Angel cracked her knuckles. "This'll be easy."

"Frankie and Lulu told me about those guys," Algie said. "They're security guards, and they seem pretty tough."

"We must utilize the element of surprise." With a final touch to her hat, Mrs. Emsworth took Algie's elbow. "Come along, darling."

Leaving Angel and Everett in the shadow of the rustling stego-saurus, Algie and his mother stepped onto the dock. As they drew within earshot of the *Dancer*, Mrs. Emsworth began to scream.

"Help! Fire! Murder! Police!"

She had a fine, operatic voice. Algie fought not to cover his ears.

"What's going on?" Both guards came to the side of the ship.

"Come quickly!" Mrs. Emsworth hoisted Algie onto the dock railing closest to the *Dancer*. "The monster is rampaging in the swim hall!"

"The professor will have to handle it," said the guard named Lenny. "We can't leave the airship. Mr. Davenport's orders.

"Mr. Davenport?" Algie wobbled on his perch. "Don't you mean Professor Champion?"

"Mr. Davenport stationed us here while he's gone," said Gabe. "Doesn't trust his daughters around the airship. Afraid they'll damage it or make off with it if they get the chance."

"We can't notify the professor," Mrs. Emsworth called. "The monster has already eaten him."

"Try O'Conner, then." Gabe was stubborn.

"We need the airship!" Algie yelled. Mrs. Emsworth grabbed at him, but he side-stepped. "We've got to rescue Frankie and Lulu!"

"So you are after the ship." Lenny adjusted his bandanna. "It wouldn't be the first time those girls cooked up a hullabaloo to fool us. The boss isn't here, and his order stands."

Two more heads popped over the railing, clambering up the mooring lines on the far side of the airship. It was Angel and Everett.

Everett flew at Lenny in his best football tackle, while Angel cartwheeled across the deck. Her twirling ribbon flashed through the air. Two seconds later, Gabe was trussed like a fly in a multi-colored spider's web.

But Angel hadn't banked on the guard's reflexes. Yanking backward, Gabe jerked the ribbon wand out of her hand and hurled himself at her knees. Angel jumped over him, and Gabe rolled away. He unraveled himself, grabbed a coiled rope, and shook out a lasso.

"Come on!" Everett yelled to Algie. He yanked a line, and the rope ladder tumbled to the water.

Algie dove into the spring and swam for the ladder. It was easier to climb than expected—he wasn't even wheezing when he reached the top.

Lenny lay hogtied in ribbons with Angel sitting atop him. Everett advanced on Gabe, who was slowly twirling his rope. Everett dove, but Gabe's lasso whirled through the air. It cinched Everett's arms to his chest. Unable to catch himself, Everett crashed to the boards.

Gabe jumped and grabbed a line of the airship's rigging. Nimbly, he scrambled upward until he clung just beneath the balloon. He unsheathed a machete from his belt and held it to the canopy.

"I don't want to slash this," he said, "but you're not making off with this craft while she's under my protection."

The airship reeled sideways.

Angel yelled as she and Lenny skidded down the slanting deck. Algie grabbed the rail, his stomach lurching.

"Bon voyage," Mrs. Emsworth called from below as she loosened the last of the *Dancer*'s mooring ropes.

Freed from her bonds, the *Dancer* bounced into the air. She lurched, caught the wind, and rolled. Gabe lost his grip and fell splashing into the spring. The wind grabbed the airship and whisked it across the lawn. Everyone was thrown into the angle of the railing. Angel hooked the rail with her leg to keep herself and Lenny from being flung overboard.

"Algie!" Everett yelled. The end of the lasso was tangled in the ship's wheel, keeping the noose around his arms cinched tight.

Algie did not have time to be scared. The airship was careering toward the hotel. Crawling along the railing, he held on with one arm and pulled out his pocketknife. His hands shook as he sawed through the rope.

Snap! The last fibers gave way. Shaking off the noose, Everett caught the dangling rope and clambered to the ship's wheel. He grabbed the spokes and spun. Everyone fell sideways again as the *Dancer* rolled in the opposite direction.

Everett let go with one hand and yanked the airship's throttle. The enormous fan engines bellowed into the wind. The *Flying Dancer* shuddered and turned—mere yards from the decorative spiked ironwork lining the hotel's courtyard walls.

"Algie! Everett!" Mrs. Emsworth ran across the lawn, leaping and stumbling over fallen palm branches. Her hat bowled backward through the grass. Everett cut the throttle and lowered the airship until its keel brushed the topiary.

"We're all right, Mother," Algie called, while Angel hooked the hogtied Lenny to the winch and lowered him over the side.

"I thought I'd killed you." Mrs. Emsworth brushed away tears. White and shaking, she looked more like the mother Algie was used to seeing. But now he understood that what he saw might not be everything.

"You were stupendous, Mother," Everett yelled.

"We've got to go," Algie shouted. The airship shivered under the strain of staying put. "Frankie and Lulu—"

"I know." Mrs. Emsworth hugged herself. "I wouldn't have raised you any other way."

"We'll be back before you know it," Algie called, as the airship whirled away over the swamp.

CHAPTER

37

"I CAN'T BELIEVE we commandeered an airship," Algie said.

"Incorrect." Standing at the wheel with rumpled clothes and hair blown every which way, Everett looked less dignified but somehow older than usual. "All the credit goes to Mother. I didn't know she had it in her."

"Neither did I." Algie was starting to believe there was more in most people, for better or worse, than he had ever suspected.

Caterpillars of white foam crawled across the rippling sea. The airship was outpacing the wind. Judging from the dark clouds streaming behind them, they were moving at a valiant clip. Everett spat, and Algie watched the glob sail sideways on the wind, down and down, until it became lost in the gulf of air.

He knelt and wiggled his fingers between the slats of the orange crate that served as Pulpy's makeshift travel container.

"Remember," he said, "your job is to stay put."

"Circus ho!" Angel called.

Madam Maximus's ship, the *Spangled Siren*, was driving along with the oblique breakers.

Angel leaned against the rail. "There's your octopus."

Algie pulled out his spyglass and directed it toward the *Siren*'s stern. A chain-link fishing net dangled over the deck. Inside huddled Octavia, lumped into a ball. Her eyes were shut. An acrobat stood beside her, holding the professor's wicked-looking tranquilizer gun. Fear stabbed Algie's heart. How long had Octavia been out of the water?

"Is she alive?" Angel shielded her eyes, squinting against the strands of loose hair whipping her face.

Algie refocused his spyglass. Between the tossing of both the *Siren* and the *Dancer*, he couldn't tell whether Octavia was moving. What would happen to Pulpy and the other babies if she were dead? Algie had no idea how to be an octopus parent.

A shout floated up from the crow's nest of the *Siren*. A uniformed acrobat, twinkling in the lowering light, signaled to the deck.

"Prepare to engage." Everett gripped the helm as a blast of wind attempted to shake the airship from its course.

"Remember our plan, Algie," Angel shouted over the rigging's whine. "And no matter what, don't take your hand off the brake rope."

Algie fumbled with the buckles of his aerialist's harness, but the buffeting airship knocked him off his feet. Balancing like a sea captain, Angel walked over and yanked the harness tight.

"Here comes trouble," Everett called.

A glittering platoon of acrobats crept upward through the *Siren*'s rigging. Angel picked up an anchor, her knuckles whitening on the chain.

Everett turned the helm and bore down on the *Siren* as if he meant to ram its crow's nest. Angel swung her anchor in slow circles. Faster and faster it looped, until *fwizz*—it shot over the side and snagged the *Siren*'s rigging.

Angel hefted a second anchor.

"Now," she yelled to Algie.

Algie gripped the rail. His knees wobbled. The ocean seemed a million miles below, the ship a ridiculously small target. Already acrobats were swarming the anchor rope. Angel let fly with her second anchor and hit a trapeze artist in the stomach. The acrobat fell but snagged a line on her way down and swooped back into the fray. Angel flung the anchor again and caught it on the crow's nest.

"Tension," she called to Everett.

His mind blank, Algie climbed onto the railing and jumped.

CHAPTER

38

ANGEL'S WORDS ECHOED through Algie's mind in place of a scream. *No matter what, don't take your hand off the brake rope.*

He fell twenty feet and hit the end of his slack. *WHAM.* His harness snatched him around the middle, and the brake rope was yanked from his hand. Algie's stomach sailed out his ears as he began to plummet again. He groped to regain his grip, but the rope leaped and jerked, zinging through the carabiner on his harness so quickly he could feel the metal heat up against his stomach. If he could not catch that rope, he would zip all the way down and straight off the end, to disappear in the ocean or smash on the deck of the *Siren*. The ship grew larger. Algie could see the tail end of his rope, dancing below.

His right hand grasped the brake rope. A white line of pain seared his palm as friction burned his skin. Algie yelped but tightened his grip.

The rope resisted—slowed, and stopped. Algie dangled over the ocean, twenty feet in the air.

Breathe. Control the line. Algie ran Angel's instructions through his head. Even in his imagination, her matter-of-fact voice steadied him. He lowered himself a little farther, until only ten feet remained between him and the end of the rope. The *Siren* was still a short distance off. He would have to swing for it.

Dusk had fallen. In the dimness above, Everett pulled the airship back so the anchor ropes drew tight. A shimmering figure walked through the air across one of them—Angel in her spangled uniform. So far, the acrobats were too preoccupied to notice Algie's dangling form.

Pump and kick. Algie leaned backward in his harness and started to swing. Slowly he picked up momentum, until he was streaking through the air. The *Siren*'s deck flashed beneath him. He let go with both hands and zipped off the end of the rope. His feet hit the deck. His legs buckled.

As if on cue, a thunderclap pounded the atmosphere. Fat raindrops spattered the deck, splashing the backs of Algie's hands.

Regaining his feet, Algie ducked behind a mast. He pulled off his dark pants and jacket, stashed his knapsack beneath them, and stood up resplendent in the bodysuit of an Aerial Acrobat. Out of habit he reached for his umbrella hat. His fingers met only the sequined mask.

Twinkling, Algie strode toward Octavia's guard.

"They want you aloft," he shouted above the rain sizzling off the deck. "I'll take over."

"She'll need another dose soon." The acrobat shot a nervous glance at Octavia. "She opened her eyes a minute ago."

"I'll take care of it." Algie held out his hand for the tranquilizer gun. The acrobat passed it to him, along with an ammunition pouch of darts.

"Don't use more than you have to," she warned. "We'll all be in trouble if we run out."

Aboard the airship, Everett pulled out his golf clubs. He hurled a putter, and a contortionist toppled from his perch. A would-be boarding party scattered to avoid the next club.

"Looks like they do need help." The acrobat scurried up the mast.

Algie shouldered the gun with rain-slick hands.

"It's me," he whispered to Octavia. "I'm going to get rid of these darts." He raised the gun, aimed to the left of the net, and fired. Octavia did not move. Algie hoped he hadn't hit her by accident.

A massive figure emerged from a hatch nearby, scarlet and gold in the dying light—Madam Maximus.

"Haven't they taken care of those ruffians yet? Hubert!"

Hubert the Strongman clambered from the hatch, twisting his shoulders to fit through the opening.

"Go aloft and instruct the others to use as much force as necessary," Madam commanded. "If the professor has resorted to piracy for these animals, I assure you he'll waste no mercy on us." She turned to Algie as Hubert lumbered off. "Give me that gun and go help them."

Algie was afraid to look at her, but the rain and darkness were on his side. Madam did not notice anything.

"I'll need the darts too," she said. "Hurry up!"

Algie fingered the pouch but was spared further indecision. Behind Madam Maximus, Octavia's eyes flew open. She flexed eight muscular arms. The chain-link net squealed.

"Shoot!" Madam ordered, backing away. Algie raised the gun to his shoulder and pulled the trigger. *Click*. Nothing happened.

"It's not working," he said. The *ping* of popping chain links obscured his voice.

Madam snatched the gun. "It's not loaded, you fool! Give me those darts!"

Whisking the ammo bag out of her reach, Algie dove to the side. Madam roared with fury and charged after him, then dodged as a sucker-lined arm burst through the net. Metal screamed and tore as Octavia ripped free. Algie crawled behind the mast that concealed his knapsack and dumped the bag of darts overboard.

Octavia slithered out of the net's remains and grabbed the empty tranquilizer gun. She ripped it from Madam's grasp and flung it into the ocean.

A ripple of concern swept the acrobats in the rigging. Half of them zipped back down to the deck, but Octavia's flailing arms kept them at bay. Algie could tell she was still groggy from the tranquilizer.

Madam Maximus stooped. She straightened up holding a long, gleaming object with a rope attached to one end.

Algie's stomach dropped. It was a whaler's harpoon.

Madam Maximus hoisted the weapon and drove it into Octavia's arm.

The octopus could not scream, and the soundlessness of the scene only increased its horror. Madam jerked the barbed harpoon free and stabbed another of Octavia's arms. Octavia swung at her tormenter. Madam dodged.

Groggily, Octavia pounced at Madam and missed. Madam jerked the rope attached to the harpoon, but Octavia grabbed her ankle with an unwounded arm. Madam's head banged the deck as Octavia pulled her into the air.

BOOM.

A group of acrobats scattered, fingers in their ears. Algie glimpsed a puff of smoke, a wooden gun carriage, and a leering metal barrel. A cannon.

Madam Maximus dropped to the planking as Octavia reeled, her arms thrashing. One of them—the one that had held Madam—was twisted and mangled. Splashes of blue blood smeared the deck.

Algie yelled, but his voice was drowned by battle cries in the rigging. Using the harpoon as a lever, Madam Maximus regained her feet. She raised the weapon and plunged it into Octavia. Twisting and writhing, Octavia raised her functioning arms to try to pull the harpoon free. Slowly, she peeled backward off the ship and fell into the tossing sea. Yards of rope spooled after her, attached to the barbed harpoon.

Rain and tears wet Algie's face, but he knew he couldn't wait any longer. He cast a final glance overhead and saw Angel balanced on her makeshift tightrope. She had managed to disarm the whip-cracker and was brandishing his weapon skillfully. Shredded clouds raced across the moon.

Madam's back turned toward Algie as she advanced to reel in her prey. Algie grabbed his knapsack and darted down the hatch.

CHAPTER

39

AS HE DESCENDED into the lamp-lit underdeck regions, Algie tried to erase the image of Octavia's terror and confusion. Warm air and the smell of tar enveloped him.

He came out in a long room swaying with hammocks. No sign of Frankie or Lulu—no sign of anyone. Algie gazed desperately around. The jail on board ship was called the brig, right? Where was the brig?

Muffled angry voices rose at the far end of the room. They seemed to be coming through the floorboards. Algie ran toward the sound and tumbled down another ladder into a storage hold.

"Who's there?" An acrobat jumped from the barrel he'd been sitting on. Behind him loomed an iron-barred door.

"They need you on deck," Algie gasped. "Angel's trying to sink us."

The guard raced past Algie and vanished. Algie ran to the brig door and tore off his mask.

"Algie!" Lulu had a scratch across one cheek but looked otherwise unharmed. "Madam said she'd killed you."

"She thought she had."

"Nice outfit." Frankie was white beneath her tan. In the half-light, her blue eyes looked black.

"Where are the keys?" Algie asked.

"On Madam's belt. I don't know where she is . . . " Lulu's voice trailed off. Frankie growled low in her throat.

Madam stood on the ladder behind Algie. Her hands were stained blue.

"Always underfoot," she said. "I should have known it was you."

Algie's knapsack wriggled against his shoulders. Pulpy! He must have escaped his orange crate and stowed away. Algie backed against the brig so his torso blocked the bag from Madam's sight.

"I don't care how you got out of that den. It doesn't matter." Rung by rung, Madam descended into the hold. Algie's knapsack squirmed harder. Pulpy was muscling free.

Algie dropped the knapsack and bolted for the door behind the ladder. Madam's whip curled around his boot. He crashed face-first into the corner.

But he had achieved his goal. Madam faced him now. Her back was toward the cell.

Algie looked her in the eyes and pretended she was a frightened octopus.

"You don't have to do this," he said.

Pulpy emerged from the knapsack behind Madam. Would the girls catch on? Yes—Frankie's hands slipped through the bars and lifted Pulpy to the lock.

"We've been over this already." Madam fingered an iron key. Her shiny boot heels clicked as she took another step.

"How do you know this new medicine will work?" Algie asked, stalling for time.

"I don't," Madam said. "But I have no other options."

"It's not worth it," Algie said. "Hurting people isn't worth it. It's better to be sick."

"What do you know about it?" Madam sneered.

"A lot." Algie was hardly aware of what he was saying. Out of his peripheral vision, he saw the bolt to the brig door slide back. Lulu was untying her sash.

Madam frowned. "What do you mean?" she asked.

"I have lung problems," Algie said. "Asthma. Maybe tuberculosis. I know lots about lying awake at night, wondering if I'll die tomorrow. But anyone can have an accident. Anyone can get hurt. No matter who you are, all you can do is . . . do your best with the day you have."

Algie could not believe it. Madam Maximus seemed to be considering his words. Was it the fact that he also was sick? That

224

didn't seem logical, seeing as how she had already tried to murder him once that day. Then again, people were not always logical.

Madam came back to herself with a start.

"Sound advice," she said. "But you won't get the chance to put it into further practice. As soon as we sink your airborne entourage, I'm chumming the water and tossing you to the sharks." She reached to grab Algie's collar.

It was the moment Algie had waited for. He threw himself forward and rammed his whole weight against Madam's chest. Caught off guard, she staggered backward and crashed through the unlocked brig door. Her knees hit the sash Frankie and Lulu held strung across the opening like a tripwire.

Madam toppled to the ground.

Algie jumped off her, grabbed the keyring, and leaped free as Lulu and Frankie slammed the door. Madam crashed into the bars, but not before Algie had clanked the bolt home.

"You'll pay for this!" Spit flew from Madam's mouth, and bars of shadow striped her face like a deranged clown's.

Algie ran to the barrel the guard had been sitting on and pried off the lid. Sure enough, seven baby octopi swam circles within. He replaced the lid before they could swarm the sides.

Madam kicked the bars and cursed.

"Let's get out of here," Frankie said.

As they heaved the barrel up the ladder, Algie paused on the top step. What was that sound?

Madam Maximus was crying.

★

Outside, the rain had stopped. The deck was deserted. Splashes of liquid, black in the moonlight, marked the site of Madam and Octavia's battle. A massive severed octopus arm lay sprawled across the planking.

"That's not—" Lulu's voice rose to a frightened pitch. "Madam didn't—"

Algie nodded.

Lulu's eyes filled with tears. Frankie said nothing but flexed her hand as though she wished it was gripping Madam's neck.

A flash of orange and a BANG sang out, this time from the airship. Smoke glowed weirdly as it blew across the moon. Acrobats decorated the rigging.

"He's got a cannon aboard that thing?" Frankie tilted her head.

"I wouldn't put anything past Professor Champion," Algie said. "I'd hardly put anything past anyone these days."

An acrobat sprang aboard the airship. Simultaneously, one of the two grappling anchors swung free. A triumphant roar arose from the troupe.

Algie spotted a lifeboat at the ship's stern. He and Lulu climbed inside the small craft while Frankie lowered it to the water. An orange glow lit the *Siren*, casting strange shadows from mast and bulwark.

Lulu screamed. "The airship is on fire!"

A fresh explosion, and more flames burst out. Angel sprinted along her anchor chain and leaped onto the *Dancer*. The anchor swung free. A fire dancer pumped her fist in the air as the victorious troupe cheered. Angel ran to and fro aboard the airship, beating at the fire. Where was Everett? Algie strained his eyes but caught no sign of him.

Waves surged, and Frankie dropped into the lifeboat as its weight transferred to the water. The tossing shadows, the salty post-storm damp, the weird glare from the airship's spotlights — all would have wrung a surge of adventure from Algie's heart if it hadn't ached so unbearably. Octavia . . . Everett's missing figure aboard the airship . . . even the image of Madam as he last saw her, crying alone in the brig. Despite everything, Algie could not write Madam off as a soulless villain. He knew what it meant to feel alone and afraid.

Lightning slashed the sky, and the ocean seemed to pulse. Algie grabbed the boat's sides for balance as Frankie raised the oars.

"Which direction, Captain?" she asked.

"It doesn't matter. Away." Fear solidified in Algie's throat. Constricting bands tightened his chest. Not an asthma attack, not now . . . He drew a wheezing breath as Frankie pulled away from the *Siren* with long, sure strokes.

Another lightning flash. Algie sucked in his breath. Something was wrong — very wrong. He had the dizzy sensation of rushing backward away from himself, unable to brake.

"What?" Frankie asked sharply. "Are you all right? Do you need your inhaler?"

Algie nodded. Frankie took the knapsack from his wobbly hands and found the asthma ball. He pressed it to his mouth and took two deep breaths.

"I saw—" he said, once he could speak.

"What?" Frankie snapped, when he paused again. "Finish your sentences. You're scaring Lulu."

Algie groped for words. What had he seen? Movement. Like the entire ocean was drawing itself together in fury.

"There's something in the water," he said.

The ocean exploded.

CHAPTER

40

THE BOAT ROCKED. Everyone ducked as seawater rained on their heads.

Algie recovered first. Wiping the hair out of his eyes, he blinked away the salt but still could not take in what he saw. Lulu had been thrown to the bottom of the boat. Frankie sat transfixed, her oars lifted.

Black, sucker-lined arms rose from the sea, thicker than tree trunks and much, much taller. Almost to the height of the *Spangled Siren*'s crow's nest they rose, and then folded back down with the ship at their center. The sea was avenging its own.

"Father Octopus," Algie breathed. Beside him, Frankie was shaking.

"The kraken," she said.

Screams erupted from the circus troupe on board the ship. Those on deck leaped back into the rigging, climbing as high as possible to get away from the arms wrapping the *Siren* in an inexorable embrace.

Aloft, the airship came about.

"They're turning back," Lulu said. "They're going to rescue them!"

Realization smacked into Algie. His whole being shuddered away from it—but he knew what he had to do.

"Go," he said to Frankie.

Frankie didn't move. Lulu snatched the oars and began to row, driving the lifeboat away from the turbulent water. Streams of acrobats piled aboard the airship as the *Siren*'s masts swayed and rocked.

Frankie had not blinked since the kraken's appearance. She was muttering under her breath.

"—seven, no, eight arms visible—" as the eighth burst from the water, "—black coloration, apparent attack on the aggressor of its family—probably a strong social bond like the female of its species—"

"Frankie," Algie said. "Frankie. FRANKIE."

"What?"

"Wait until the acrobats are on board the airship, and then fire a second shot."

"What are you talking about?"

For answer, Algie reached into his knapsack and pulled out the *Diving Belle*'s flare pistol. He cocked it in the air, covered his ears with his free hand and shoulder, and fired. Red light streaked skyward, scattering sparks over the seascape.

Frankie jumped backward at the bang. Algie thrust the flare gun into her hand, taking care to keep the barrel pointed away from anyone. The thought came that if he disappeared beneath these waves, his dreams died with him.

It didn't matter. He knew who, not what, he wanted to be. Words from a quiet fireside flashed across his mind.

I will die with my face to the sun.

"Your ship now, Captain," he said to Frankie, and dove into the ocean.

★

It was dark beneath the water—much darker than the first time he'd fallen into that sparkling, sunlit sea. But this time Algie was not helpless. He rose to the surface and kicked into a breast-stroke. Water sloshed around him as he reached the ship's side.

A wave surged over his head. Algie relaxed and let his body swirl under. When the swell passed, he bobbed to the surface. Another wave slapped his face. Battling turbulence, he swam toward one of the huge, trunk-like arms.

There was enough space between suckers gripped to the hull that Algie could climb them like a ladder—a moving, writhing, terrifying ladder of muscle. Despite his constricting airway, he made it to the bulwark. His hand grasped the railing.

231

The ship rolled. Algie's feet slipped and swung outward. The *Siren* surged in the other direction, and he slammed against the hull. A sucker-lined arm towered over him as the kraken tightened its grip. Timbers groaned and railings splintered. The arm was almost on him—it would squash him into jelly and never know it.

Algie threw a leg onto the deck. He climbed hand over hand up the rail slats and flung himself out of harm's way as the kraken's arm slammed down. He rolled without losing momentum and was up again, running. The hatch to the crew's quarters loomed in front of him.

The deck bucked. Algie flew through the hatch. Midair, he managed to twist so that he landed on his shoulder. Pain slammed through the back of his head.

The passageway slanted as the ship stood on end. Algie got to his feet. Sliding from hammock to hammock, he staggered down the slope.

Not a scream or sound issued from the hold. Algie half-fell down the ladder.

Madam Maximus crouched in the lowest corner of the brig, hands over her eyes. Her lips moved.

"I'm sorry," Madam Maximus was saying. "I'm sorry, I'm sorry . . ."

"Madam!" Algie yelled.

Madam's head jerked up.

"You're a ghost," she said. "Come back to punish me."

"You've been reading too much Godric Featheringstone III."

Algie coughed, pounding his chest with a fist. He shoved the key into the door and pulled it open.

By now the ship slanted so the floor was almost a wall. Algie and Madam fought upward through the crew's quarters, holding on by anything they could grip.

Crash. Crash.

A heavy barrel bounded toward them, smashing woodwork as it came. It cannoned into a support beam and ricocheted toward Algie.

Madam Maximus flung herself into its path.

Thunk. The barrel reeled off and Madam fell backward. Her right arm hung at a strange angle.

"Go!" she shouted, forestalling Algie's words.

Even with one arm, Madam managed the second ladder better than Algie. Every breath felt as though he had to suck it through a tiny straw, and each one took more muscle. He squeezed a gulp of salt air as they emerged on deck.

The ship's entire stern was underwater. At its base swirled an immense black body. White waves broke around the kraken's bulk, gleaming in the moonlight. Two red eyes glared from the water, fixed unblinkingly on the ship.

Algie glanced around, but everything movable had toppled overboard long ago. Madam's face was pale. Sweat glistened on her forehead and rolled down her collar.

"We'll—figure—something—out." Algie could barely breathe. He knew Madam couldn't swim with her injured arm, and he would not be able to keep her above water. They had to find a flotation device. A glance over his shoulder revealed the airship touching down on the water beneath the smoke of Frankie's second flare.

A shrieking crack ricocheted through the night. The ship began to slide under. Faster, faster—

Madam and Algie raced to the side and flung themselves into the gulf.

CHAPTER

41

KOOSH.

Any hope of regaining the surface was knocked from Algie's body along with his last bit of breath. His arms were spaghetti, his legs useless logs of wood. No oxygen remained in his lungs. Madam Maximus's words swam through his muzzy brain. *I'm sorry.*

Something wrapped around his waist. Algie was drawn upward, faster and faster. Maybe this was dying—shooting through space until he burst into another existence. He could not hold his breath any longer.

Algie inhaled as he shot into the air. His asthma still gripped him, but he was breathing. And somehow not dead, but suspended above water. He looked down.

A sucker-lined arm was twined around his waist, holding him up and supporting his head. A pink arm, dappled with calm rings of lavender. Rippling through the velvet sea, gazing at him through barred eyes deep with the ocean's peace—swam Octavia! A short way distant, she held another form aloft: bulky, waterlogged, and hatless, but still clutching her ringmistress's whip—Madam Maximus.

Algie could not speak, but he didn't want to. Waves of thankfulness crashed into his chest.

Octavia lifted him over the railing and laid him on the floating airship's deck. Ranks of awed, silent acrobats drew apart as she placed Madam Maximus beside him. Everett was there, one arm wrapped in a makeshift bandage and his eyebrows singed off. Angel, too, looked like she had been through a riot.

Smoke-blackened and shaky, Everett lifted his uninjured hand as Octavia's arm passed by.

"She won't mind if you touch her," Lulu said.

Everett's fingers brushed Octavia as the great octopus withdrew overboard.

A round object thumped into Algie's chest. He caught it automatically. Frankie stood over him with Pulpy perched on her shoulder. Monday and Tuesday nestled in Lulu's arms, and the other babies had found friends among the troupe. Sunday was wrapped around Hubert's head like a slimy bishop's mitre.

"Shouldn't you use that?" Frankie nodded to the object she had thrown. It was Algie's inhaler.

Algie breathed in, medicine tickling his throat. The knot in his chest loosened.

Everett, Angel, and Lulu—even the circus troupe—began to wave. Leaning forward, Algie saw Octavia wiggling her arms. Only seven. The eighth arm was gone.

"She must have—shed it," Algie murmured between wheezes. "She shed her—injured arm—like the earthworm shed its tail."

Madam Maximus heaved herself upright and lifted her good arm in salute.

"Glad to see you." Everett thumped Algie's shoulder. "We thought you went down with the ship. I—" Embarrassed, he broke off, strode to the wheel, and opened the throttle. The great brass fan roared to life.

But the laden airship made slow headway against the wind and choppy waves.

"I don't think we'll be able to lift off with all this weight." Everett scratched his jaw. "It's going to be a long ride home."

"I know what will help get us back," Madam Maximus said.

"How do we know you won't sabotage us?" Everett asked.

"It's all right," Algie said. "You can trust her."

Assisted by Hubert and Angel, Madam Maximus came to the control panel and flipped a combination of switches. A score of golden oars shot from the airship's sides. They dipped, pulled, and rose, flashing and feathering in unison. A whirring hum rumbled up through the deck—the gear song of the mechanical galley.

Half an hour later, dressed in a spare set of clothes from his dry bag, Algie sat wedged in the front of the boat behind the figurehead. The rhythmic surge of waves made his eyelids droop.

Frankie dropped to sit cross-legged beside him.

"I'm sorry I said being nice doesn't matter," she said.

"I beg your pardon?"

"I always thought," Frankie leaned back on her palms, "that treating nasty people nicely was a sign of weakness. But maybe it's the opposite."

Algie fidgeted with his shirt hem.

"I was also thinking," said Frankie, "that once we get back, we could all start taking turns being captain."

"That's a good idea," Algie said. "Take a vote at the beginning of each expedition to decide who's most qualified."

"Speaking of expeditions, we still need to get those octopuses to Cuba. Madam Maximus may have given up, but there's always Professor Champion and Papa."

"We will," Algie said. "I have a plan."

For once, Frankie did not cross-examine or boss. Instead, she stretched her legs in front of her.

"Aye-aye, Captain," she said. "By the way, did you ever notice that that figurehead looks a lot like Madam Maximus?"

Octavia kept pace beside the ship, unbothered by her missing arm. A crested ripple gleamed around her mantle as she swam.

"Is that wave glowing?" Algie asked.

"Bioluminescent plankton," Frankie said. "You know, I almost want to be mad at you for rescuing us. Normally, I like to be the one who does all the rescuing."

"Blame Pulpy," Algie said. "He rescued you, not me."

"True," Frankie said. "And I did rescue you from Jasper that one time. Sort of."

"And Octavia rescued Algie from the alligator," said Lulu, sitting down on Algie's other side. "And Algie's mother rescued Angel from Professor Champion."

Frankie shook her head. "I've been falling behind on the rescuing business."

"I think we could all use a little rescuing now and then," Lulu said. "To keep our heads on straight. There's nothing wrong with needing help."

The wave around Octavia shone brighter and brighter. So did the wave from the *Dancer*'s bow. Algie looked behind and saw their wake, glowing green behind them.

"I could sing right now," Frankie said.

"I think we've been through enough tonight," Algie said, and dodged as she whacked him.

CHAPTER

42

A BLUSTERY GOLDEN afternoon some days later, Algie, Lulu, and Frankie stepped off the *Flying Dancer*'s rope ladder. Professor Champion leaned his elbows on the balustrade.

"Thanks, Professor," Algie said.

"It's painful to let those exquisite specimens slip through my fingers, but I think they'll enjoy their new home. Oh, don't worry—I know I said I wouldn't rest until I'd pickled them all in formaldehyde, but this is one time Professor Ransom Champion will have to eat his words." He stroked his false side-whiskers. "I can't say I like the taste though."

"I trust *you*," Frankie said to Algie, "but why are you so certain we can trust *him*?" She jabbed a thumb toward the professor.

"I wouldn't normally advise it," said the professor. "Trusting me, that is. But on this occasion, young lady, you may set your mind at rest. Madam Maximus and I have been—acquainted—for a long time. I would be deeply distressed had a kraken swallowed her."

Frankie raised an eyebrow.

"Magnificent woman," the professor murmured. "Such presence." He gazed misty-eyed at a passing flock of sandpipers. "The number of times I've begged her to accept my hand in marriage . . . but she never will. Thinks I'm too stubborn to make a comfortable husband. She's right, of course. Sometimes I wonder how things would have turned out if I'd been more willing to compromise . . . but it's too late to change."

"It's never too late to change," Algie said.

The professor laughed. "You'll know better when you're my age."

"No, he won't," Lulu said. "Even when he's your age, he'll never be you."

Surprisingly, the professor did not seem angry.

"Maybe you're right," he said. "Well, give my best to your father. I hope I won't be seeing you again."

"Where are you going?" Algie asked.

"Mexico. There've been reports of a giant flying lizard carrying off donkeys in the Sierra del Tigre. I've convinced the collector to sponsor an expedition."

"Who is this collector, anyway?" Frankie asked.

"If you knew, you'd start interfering again," said the professor. "And I secured a promise from Madam Maximus not to tell, so it's no use appealing to her. Goodbye."

The *Flying Dancer* lifted off. As it set out over the Gulf of Mexico, a bang and puff of smoke from the cannon signaled the professor's final salute.

When the smoke had dissipated and clouds hid the airship, the three children walked back up the pier. Algie stayed quiet on the tram ride through the swamp. The trees and twisting shadows that had seemed so ominous on his arrival were now familiar friends. The vines and air plants weren't light-blotting parasites, but a cool screen to shield him from the sun.

Outside the hotel, Everett and Parker James sat at a table beneath the coconut grove.

"Successful mission?" Everett hailed the returning travelers.

For her answer, Lulu laid down a sketch she had water-colored on the return journey. It showed an isolated cove fringed with emerald bushes. White clouds like mountains towered over distant hills.

"We finally got to see Cuba," she said. "I'm going back to paint it."

"You might get caught in a war," Parker warned.

"We'll help fight it." Frankie twirled an imaginary revolver. "Cuba libre."

"You don't think the octopi will come back?" Everett asked. "It's not that far for a big animal to swim."

"Not until the red tide is over," Algie said. "But by then, everyone will be gone."

"What about next season?"

The clatter of palm fronds filled the silence.

"There won't be a next season." Lulu tipped her chin. "Papa met with his advisers. The hotel is still losing money, so he decided to shut it down."

"That's a shame," Everett said. "I was starting to like the place."

"He isn't selling the property," Frankie said. "He's thinking about maintaining one of the smaller buildings as a private summerhouse. Maybe you can come visit."

Algie imagined the jungle creeping across the lawn, extending its tendrils and punching out the greenhouse glass, taking over the hotel.

A tall figure in athletic bloomers strode from the courtyard, waving a piece of paper.

"Letter from Madam," Angel called as she neared the group.

"What does she say?" Everett asked.

"Since the victims asked for leniency, the judge let her off with ten years' imprisonment for two charges of kidnapping and one of attempted murder. Hubert's taking over the circus, and part of Madam's sentence will be to help organize benefit shows for prison-reform charities. And—" Angel's cheeks were pinker than usual, the hard look gone from her face "—she dissolved my contract. I'm free."

Everett flushed as well. "I say, Angel—would you like to take a walk?"

"I've got to pack," Angel said. "I'm leaving tomorrow morning."

"Five minutes?"

Angel laughed. "Whatever you're dying to say, you might as well save time and have it out now. What's eating you?"

"Nothing! I—" Everett glared at Lulu, who was giggling. "Hang it, Angel, when am I going to see you again?"

"You're welcome to come see us in Colorado," Parker said.

Angel put her hand on Parker's.

"I guess you haven't heard," she said. "Parker and I are getting married. We've been engaged for over a year."

"But I thought you didn't like him," Algie said, once it became clear that Everett was incapable of speech.

"I know I said that," Angel admitted. "But I thought—didn't you see us in the greenhouse the other day, Algie? Anyway, I told Madam we broke it off. I owe you one for that, Ev. I thought if I spent more time with you, it'd get Madam to lay off Parker a bit. She was always shouting at him."

Parker slapped Everett's shoulder. "Sorry for pulling the wool over your eyes, old man. But we figured you'd understand."

A strangled gurgle escaped Everett's throat. It satisfied Parker and Angel, though.

"You're a pal." Angel beamed at Everett. "And a good kid. You all are. And you've all got to visit once we're settled out West. We're thinking of going into the mustang-gentling busi-

ness. Once I finish my new book, that is! I decided on a title—
The Slithey Sea Serpent of Seawinds Castle."

"That sounds wonderful!" said Algie. He elbowed Everett.

"Wonderful," Everett mumbled.

"Maybe we can meet up at a different hotel next season," said Parker. Angel nodded.

"I bet Algie could help me if I get writer's block again," she said. "He sees things other people don't."

"I do?" Algie was astonished.

"Sure," Angel said, "Little details, and the best in people. Well, we've got a lot to do. See you around, kids." She winked at Algie, patted Everett's cheek, and waltzed away with her arm through Parker's.

"Lulu! FRANK-ie!" The call floated across the lawn.

Frankie groaned. "It's Papa. He probably wants us to pack."

"Where are you going?" Everett asked.

"Back to boarding school." Lulu sighed.

"Chin up," Frankie said. "A good naturalist can find something to fascinate anywhere. You've got those healthy seawater samples?" she asked Algie. "You didn't lose them, or let them get stolen?"

Algie held up a satchel of glass vials. Frankie looked relieved.

"Meet us at the *Belle* after dinner," she said. "We've still got a lot of work to do."

When the girls had gone, Everett and Algie sat alone at the table. A flock of ibis strutted past, poking their curved bills into the earth.

"Did you ever get that photograph back?" Everett asked. "The one with you and Octavia?"

Algie shook his head. "It went down with the ship. We could have taken another if we wanted. Madam Maximus told the newspapers her attack was a hoax, so people think the octopi never existed."

"Better that way." Everett nodded. "I'm sorry you didn't get to publish your grand discovery."

Another figure emerged from the courtyard—Mrs. Emsworth balancing in her button boots as she maneuvered through the grove. Everett pulled out a chair for her, but Mrs. Emsworth stayed standing. She brushed an ant off Everett's shoulder and straightened Algie's collar.

"How are you feeling, darling?" she asked. "Has Florida done you any good?"

Algie swallowed a tickle in his throat. There was a sea wind tonight, which always aggravated his symptoms. Soon they would leave the Hotel Paraíso, probably forever. But he had two true friends at his back, and his mother and brother by his side.

"I've never felt better," he said. "*Achoo!*"

EPILOGUE

Dear Miss Francisca Davenport, Miss María de Lourdes Davenport, and Master Algernon Emsworth,

It is my pleasure to inform you that your paper, "The Florida Red Tide: A Possible Causative Organism and Overview of its Effects on Gulf Coast Marine Life and the Human Respiratory System," has been accepted for publication.

Sincerely,

L. P. Popplewell, President

Chicago Academy of Natural History

Acknowledgments

My first debt is toward my incomparable home state, where, as writer Dave Barry observes, "We cannot rule *anything* out, because we never know what will happen next in Florida. We know only that, any minute now, *something will*." Special thanks to Harbor Branch Oceanographic Institute for nurturing my childhood love of our state's ecosystems.

To Mira Reisberg of the Children's Book Academy, thank you for connecting me with my agent, Hannah Fergesen. Huge thanks to Hannah for believing in this book when it was just a baby log line, and to my editor, Ardi Alspach, whose insights and encouragement were so very helpful.

Rob and Chris, thanks for reading the manuscript way more times than any human should have had to endure, and Johnny, for pointing out to me whenever my ideas were too boring. Thank you, Abuelita and Abuelito—although we'll never match your coolness factor, we all still want to be just like you. To the rest of my family, "thanks" doesn't cut it, but that's what you get, because I don't have space to write a whole separate book.

Forever thank you to the medical teams who saved my life and reassembled me (literally) in between this book's sale and publication. Also to my husband, Tanner, for listening whenever I'm stuck in a dark night of the writerly soul, and to my kids for requesting "your octopus book, please, Mom," as their bedtime story.

To God who is love I give thanks daily for this beautiful planet and its inhabitants.

About the Author

Samantha San Miguel grew up on the Treasure Coast of Florida. Living sandwiched between ocean and estuary gave her a whole-hearted respect for wildlife, especially the kind that can eat you. She's spent countless hours scanning for sea monsters, but the only ones she's seen so far have been in her imagination. Samantha dreams of one day seeing with her own eyes the landscapes from her abuelito's stories of Cuba.